JUNKYARD
CATS

Books by Faith Hunter

The Jane Yellowrock Series

SKINWALKER

BLOOD CROSS

MERCY BLADE

RAVEN CURSED

DEATH'S RIVAL

BLOOD TRADE

BLACK ARTS

BROKEN SOUL

DARK HEIR

SHADOW RIGHTS

COLD REIGN

THE JANE YELLOWROCK WORLD COMPANION

DARK QUEEN

SHATTERED BONDS

TRUE DEAD

FINAL HEIR

Compilations

BLOOD IN HER VEINS

OF CLAWS AND FANGS

continued...

JUNKYARD
CATS

novella 1

FAITH HUNTER

LORE
SEEKERS
PRESS

JUNKYARD CATS
ISBN 978-1-62268-175-4
Copyright © 2020 Faith Hunter

Also available in e-book form: ISBN 978-1-62268-155-6

Cover illustration by Rebecca Frank, Bewitching Book Covers.

Printed in the United States of America on acid-free paper.

Lore Seekers Press is an imprint of Bella Rosa Books.
Lore Seekers Press and logo are trademarks of Bella Rosa Books.

10   9   8   7   6   5   4   3   2   1

Acknowledgments

No book is written in a vacuum. This novella, and the entire Junkyard Cats series, has been dependent on several people.

Editor Steve Feldberg at Audible for all the wonderful suggestions and insights for the Audible Original! Every care has been taken to deviate not at all.

Agent Lucienne Diver with The Knight Agency for acquiring an Audible Original for the Junkyard Cats series. This has been such fun!

Cover design by Rebecca Frank of Bewitching Book Covers. Love it!

Robert Martin, physicist and theoretical physicist-adventurer. The creator of the science behind the WIMP engines and the EntNu communications system in the Junkyard Universe.

Bonnie Smietanowska, physicist.

Mud Mumudes for all things plant-ish and genetic-y.

Brenda Rezk for breaking down genetic stuff I couldn't understand.

Teri Lee Akar editor extraordinaire.

Let's Talk Promotions for running PR.

And to Lore Seekers Press for the e-book and print editions, thank you.

JUNKYARD
CATS

With a soft clatter, I put down the wrench and walked around my latest delivery, hands loose at my sides. I wasn't sure why I was so discomfited by the hunk of scrap. It triggered that sixth sense that had kept me alive for so long, but I couldn't tell why. Maybe I was finally being paranoid for no reason.

I rubbed my sweaty scalp, my hand sliding up under my floppy hat, studying the old AGR Tesla fuselage. The hatch was sealed with the yellow tape of military and civilian decertification, tape that marked the AntiGrav Retrofit vehicle as airtight. It also marked it legal for scrap, not that it was. Legal, that is.

Everything looked normal. But still.

I picked at the cracked orange nail polish on my fingernails, staring at the hood. Walked down one side. Uncertain. My sixth sense buzzed stronger. Maybe it was the ugly paint, a piss-poor chitosan polymer job in an unexpected hot fuchsia-pink that someone with lousy taste had sprayed over the former military gray. The vivid color made the space-worthy composite body look like a military camp follower in full hooker regalia. But. It was just paint. Nothing to make me so jittery.

I walked around the fuselage and stopped at the hatch. Stepped closer. And backed away fast. *That* was what was bothering me. There were ants skittering over the Tesla, crawling around the hatch and up over the roof as if they had found a nice meal where the vehicle had been parked, and then seen their lunch box carried away from their nest. They were mad, racing around the sun-heated metal as if the temp wasn't a problem at all. *Ants*. But not just any ants. *Cataglyphis bicolor fabricius* ants.

Over the last few years there had been any number of scrap deliveries that gave me the willies, and this 2035 AGR Tesla and its ants was at the top of the list. Fighting the natural desire to run, I took several more very slow steps back.

The ants didn't belong here, not on this Tesla, not in the stony West Virginia desert. They didn't actually belong anywhere. The bicolors had been imported from the Sahara Desert during the first year of the war, when things had gotten bad. There had been all kinds of ecological and environmental catastrophes and stupid importations and genetic modifications that the survivors were still living with. Bicolors were among the worst environmental mistakes ever created and they were nearly indestructible. The males—only the males—had been modified on the genetic level by bio-nanobots, and sent out from some top-secret lab by the millions to clean up the mounds of dead humans and eat the germs that came from the corpses. Unable to reproduce without a female, they were programmed to die at the end of their normal lifespans.

Except a few of them had absorbed some transposons from a Ginkgo biloba plant, developed sequential hermaphroditism, and figured out how to reproduce.

Their bites and stings had evolved overnight to

become lethal.

They were impossible to eradicate and mean as hell.

I know. I was swarmed and survived and had the scars to prove it.

I rejected the urge to rub my right wrist on my britches. It tingled with remembered pain, burning even though the damaged nerves had been cauterized and nothing was left of the injury except the scarring and the nightmares. Unlike my other scars, these showed, and if I was making a rare trip into the big city for supplies, I either covered them with makeup or hid them beneath a sparkly bracelet to match the girly clothes and lacy gloves and dangerous strappy shoes I got to wear once in a blue moon.

I still missed the girl I had been before the war, but staying alive was more important than pretty dresses. And since I was legally dead, I avoided cities and other people like the plagues they sometimes carried.

I took another slow step back.

I hadn't seen a bicolor in five years. My Berger-chip implant started to provide me with the usual useless data, but I tapped it off. This stuff I knew, and the only thing that mattered was that the genetically modified ants had group intelligence and killed anything that moved.

Because of the modified hermaphroditism, anytime thirteen male ants got together in one place without a queen, one would change sex and, *voila*, there was the start of a new nest. Twelve bicolors and nothing happened. Add in that thirteenth and bingo. The bio-nanobots that had created the bicolors could be transferred only by the main queen in a nest, not any secondary females born or added to the nest.

There were way more than thirteen on the scrap Tesla body. All males, the short bodies and small abdomens indicating their gender.

Bloody damn.

I pulled back on the red knob, slowly disengaging the AntiGravity Grabber. The vehicle settled gradually to the ground with a muted *whomp*. I adjusted my hat over my sweat-spiked hair and pulled on armored gauntlets that had been scavenged from an antique warbot, circa 2040. The bot had been part of the reason I had set up for business here, in the middle of nowhere. Smith's Junk and Scrap specialized in postwar surplus and waste. The discarded bot—and the half-buried, partially-intact, US spaceship on the back lot—had been too good to pass up. The junkyard "office"—an even bigger lure, once I figured out what it really was—had become my home and hideaway.

The warbot gauntlets were oversized and reached my elbows, but they worked just fine, slipping five miniscule needles under the skin of each hand to engage my peripheral nerves. It hurt like crap for about ten seconds, but I'd lost pain sensitivity at these particular insertion sites over the years, like calluses on my nerve endings.

In the machine hut, I found a half-empty gallon jug of Maltodine, a sodium-based, flammable substance made for killing any number of genetically modified creatures. Back in the sun, I made sure I was downwind of the vehicle and the ants, doused the Tesla in the gooey red toxin, and watched it spread. It was created to expand and wasn't something the ants had adapted to notice as deadly. Yet. I lit and tossed an old-fashioned match at the Tesla. The fluid whooshed into flame, instantly so hot it burned blue. On fire, it spread even faster.

The bicolors screamed in unison, a terrible, high-pitched harmonic that spoke of group intelligence and communal vengeance. "Burn, you little buggers," I muttered, watching as they rushed to try and save their pals and all burned, hot and spitting and gone. The flower-pink paint looked cheery beneath the toxic blue flames, self-healing even as the fire danced across it. The flames were pretty in my 2-Gen sunglasses as I switched back and forth between the raptor eye lenses and UV.

None of the ants made it off the Tesla's valuable graphite epoxy trusses and hemplaz carbon-fiber composite body. Not one. Relief spread through me when the last ant died.

"My sensors are picking up Maltodine fumes," Mateo said into my earbud. We were WIMP-powered, EntNu linked, the Entangled Dark Neutrinos providing instantaneous communication even had he been on the far side of the solar system.

Mateo was my employee. Sort of. I'd found the war vet working as slave labor in a town on the way here. I'd stolen him from his owner and given him a home. Mateo knew all my secrets. Every single one.

I tapped my ear and told him about the ants and my solution, and said, "Come hell or high water, I'm making money off this purchase." Unspoken was the addendum: *and a lot more money off the stolen, spanking brand-new, functional black-market Tesla-23B engine my contact had put in the back hatch, along with a couple of space-going pulse weapons.* Mateo and I knew scrap, and the AGR and its no-where-near-legal cargo were mega-valuable.

Scuttlebutt said the war was heating back up. Anyone with weapons and engines stood to make a nice profit. And anyone with military supplies, weapons, and scrap, needed to make sure it never fell into the wrong hands—the hands of traitors who were dealing with the enemy. I sold only to people in my network, people I trusted, and while those could be counted on one hand with fingers left over, this delivery already had buyers on both the legal market and my black-market network.

Mateo grunted, or as much of a grunt as his bio-metallic larynx could make, which was more like metal grinding and rubber squeaking. "Lunch is ready," he added.

Satisfied, I took a break in the air-conditioned office and ate the lunch, a cold plate Mateo left in the double-sided fridge. He was mostly cy-bot now, having lost everything below the hips, part of his face, and one arm at the shoulder. He was addicted to Devil Milk, and I grew the plants in the camouflaged greenhouse at the back of the property just for him. It was the only thing that helped the military vet's pain, and though the Gov. and the Law said Devil Milk was illegal, the local law officers weren't in pain. Mateo was. So, screw 'em. I protected my own.

I didn't use. I never would. Except for surgery, we Outlaw Militia Warriors didn't use drugs of any kind. Before and after, OMW just toughed it out. Not that the militia organization even knew I was alive anymore. But some traditions were never to be neglected. I stayed clean.

Except for beer. And a little tequila if it was the good stuff.

But not drugs. Ever.

Today's half-imported, half-homegrown, fermented delight was a lovely extra stout, dark as sin, with a head the color of caramel and a body so thick it was like sipping a milkshake. Best beer ever made, including pre-war stuff. With the beer came gourmet hummus with hot green chilies, a green salad with tomatoes, asparagus, okra, a homemade dressing of basil vinegar mixed with olive oil, and fresh bread. Just like yesterday and the day before, the veggies changing only with the growing seasons, not that I complained. Most anything was better than prepackaged ready-to-eat meals, and not many people got fresh food anymore.

As a chef, Mateo was dependable, not inventive. He lost that part of his brain along with the rest of his body parts, but I never turned away a military vet who wanted a meal, a gallon of fresh water, or a job. Never. It was part of the creed left to me by Pops, my father, who was OMW to the core.

Leaning into the NBP compression command seat, I looked over the boards and screens that ran and oversaw the junkyard's office. I breathed the air released from the leaves of the modified air-scrubber plants and watched the burning Tesla. I fanned myself with my damp floppy hat, and let the A/C cool me, drying my sweat to a crusty, salty layer of white. I ate, drank the beer and a lot of water, took several electrolyte tablets, and watched through the heavy-weapon-fire resistant window as the Maltodine burned across the exterior of the ancient AGR Tesla.

I could separate, recycle, and sell the body. The hemp tires were dry-rotted, the interior of the cockpit—what I had seen through the silk-plaz canopy—was bare to the frame, the space-worthy NBP compression seats were gone, electrical and hydro were gone. The wings had been stripped off and secured to a separate skid with military flex for easier transport. The rear engine compartment was sealed and invisible from the outside, but the weight alone told me that the Tesla-23B Massive Particle Propulsion engine I had paid extra for—a lot extra for—had been tucked into the hatch along with the weapons, just as I had been promised.

Sooo. That meant my jitters were solely from the ants—my own personal nightmare come calling. Pops had said, "Fear is a peculiar thing, love. You either run toward it, away from it, or you freeze." Yeah. I had frozen, and that was stupid in the middle of a battle.

I was always in the middle of a battle, even if it

was just the one in my head.

Half an hour later, the fire was out. I used the composting toilet, brushed my teeth, put on more 110 SPF sunscreen, and smeared on moisturizing lip gloss in a deep-orange color. Just because it was practical didn't mean it couldn't be pretty, even in the treeless, rocky West Virginia desert landscape where no one could see me.

I headed back to the Tesla. It was steaming in the day's heat as the last of the toxic fumes blew away. The mounting jacks used for the pulse weapons, the AntiGrav, and the WIMP engine were now super-heated hot-pink metal, as were the stripped weapons mounts. Using the wrench I had put aside earlier, I popped the lock, and the hatch over the rear engine compartment began to lift, ripping through the fire-proof yellow tape that marked it as sealed by various West Virginia authorities.

The black maw opened. The stench boiled out.

The engine and the weapons I'd been expecting had not been sealed inside after all.

The body in their place smiled at me. So to speak. He'd been dead a while. Most of the tissue of his lips, nose, and lids were gone, revealing tobacco-stained teeth and empty holes where his eyes had been. He was naked and mostly covered by hundreds of bicolors. I froze in place, not breathing, my heart beating so hard it felt as if it would pound through my chest.

The little scavenger predator ants would have sensed their compatriots dying, but that had been eons ago in bicolor time. They paused, evaluated the opening of the hatch and my unmoving body—which was cooler than the ambient temp—decided there were no predators, and went back to work, rushing all over the inside of the Tesla and all over the naked body. Except three spots. Two were where his tats had been inked above his heart.

On his upper pec were two black six-shooters, crossed over a gold star that still glittered with the ink the OMW had begun utilizing just after the war started in 2043—Tattered Pride Gold. Made only for the Outlaw Militia Warriors. The letters *OMW* were red and dripped down like blood onto the lower, larger tat. Touched by the last drop of red ink was an original Outlaw tat, skull and crossed Harley pistons, also free of ants.

The tats were old and faded and so was he, a war vet and an OMW made-man, mid-sixties, silvered red hair and beard, and a tattoo of Tennille Tennyson's face on his left bicep. Ants were eating away at the tat of the singer's pretty face. I knew this guy, just by his tattoos, even without running a viber over him for verification.

His name was Harlan. Buck Harlan.

He was my connection to the network, the black-market web where I bought and sold weapons and info. He and Mateo were the only people in the entire world who knew I was alive. He had been my father's friend. He was also my friend, one of only two. Something inside me broke, shattered into slivers like glass, cutting my soul. I managed a breath I had been holding too long. The ants didn't notice the slight movement.

The third part of Harlan that hadn't been attacked by bicolors was the hemp-plaz note in his swollen fingers. On the front were my initials in his messy scrawl.

The chances of Harlan showing up here, in the middle of nowhere, by accident, covered in bicolors, with a note to me in his dead fingers, were low enough to be impossible. Harlan was dead because of me. Which meant there was a traitor in the Gov. and in Harlan's network. I just didn't know who.

I swore, but silently, in my head, not where the ants could hear me. They still hadn't noticed me. Yet. I stepped back, slowly, *slowly*, moving steadily, doing nothing quick to attract attention. I pulled my Hand-Held and took a burst of the body. Walking at a snail's pace around the vehicle, I took multiple bursts of stills as I moved, until I was back at the hatch.

Moving so slow it was like watching the sun cross the sky, I slipped on the military bot gloves. But something alerted the bicolors. As the gloves gripped onto my hands and arms, the ants turned to look at me. All of them. All at once. A shiver took me, even with the heat. But I didn't scream, run, or indicate fear that might tweak their predatory instincts. Moving millimeter by millimeter, I pocketed the Hand-Held and reached for the Maltodine.

I needed to kill them.

I *needed* to read that letter.

The ants hissed. All of them together. A single sharp, piercing note. Looking right at me.

"Oh, bloody damn," I whispered.

The ants raced around, forming into small groups, each the requisite thirty-nine in number, which was three groups of thirteen. There were four groups of thirty-nine in all, with a ragged half group. Enough to start over a dozen new nests. Here. On my junkyard land.

Over my dead body.

Over Harlan's dead body.

Assuming they were a swarming party, sent to bring back food to an established nest, that meant these bicolors had been transported a good hundred kilometers from their queen; it tended to take a few hours before the ants noticed that they didn't have a female anymore. It took seventy-two hours to complete the transition to female. I didn't know how long they had been away from their nest, but they would notice they needed to create a queen soon. I had to act now.

But I *needed* that note.

"Shining. Company," Mateo's synthetic voice said directly into my wireless earbud. "Bike. Unknown model. Ten klicks out. I am launching ARVACs," he said, referring to Auto Remote Viewing Air Craft—flying drones with better-than-standard artificial intelligence and real-time viewing, part of the junkyard's defense system.

"The Law?" I whispered, looking at Harlan's body, the jug a handbreadth from my fingertips. I had no desire to be hauled in for questioning over a dead man I hadn't seen in years. But I had no desire to have ants take over my junkyard. I had no desire to be swarmed again. Remembered fear shivered down my spine like thousands of tiny ant feet.

"Unproven," he said. "One vehicle. Approaching at 54 kph. No visible backup."

No sane lawman rode anywhere alone, and never on a bike. Someone had sent Harlan's body, part of a special delivery sealed by the Gov. With bloody bicolor ants which no sane person would have done. It could *not* be simple bad luck.

Not the Law. Not the Gov. Not the military. The gift-giver was someone who wanted to play with me like a pride of cats with a junkyard dog. Or someone who knew what I really had on the property.

I opened the Maltodine and tossed the entire container in the hatch. The ants swarmed toward me.

I struck a match. Reached for the hatch door with one gloved hand. Tossed the match with the other. Lightning fast, I ripped the note away. Just before the hatch closed, intense heat boiled out, and I heard the ants scream as the sound cut off.

Maltodine burned anything anywhere, even without oxygen—except hemp-plaz composite. Maltodine didn't burn anything made of metal or hemp that had been combined with silk-plaz at the atomic level. It burned until it no longer had anything organic to fuel it. Harlan, however, was organic.

I tapped over my heart with a two fingered salute and said, "Peace, my brother. There will be no more war. May your last ride on the dragon's tail be peaceful."

I dropped my salute. "Deets on the visitor when available," I requested of Mateo. "And calculate Maltodine burn time of one hundred kilos of organic matter in an anaerobic environment."

"Copy that."

The Berger-chip implant started to provide the answer. I shut it down. Once I let that thing start talking it never shut up, and I had to sleep sometime.

With a gauntleted fist, I hammered the red ignition button and the AG Grabber came back on, the almost-imperceptible whine an itch under my skin. Initiating the controls, I maneuvered the Grabber over the top of the Tesla and lowered the unit until it almost connected. Then I raised the old war fuselage three and a half meters off the ground, the maximum ever achieved on land, even by the military of three warring groups of allied nations. AntiGrav was a misnomer on a planet surface, the moniker applied by a PR person when it was first invented, and it had stuck, even after WIMP engines had given us intra-solar system flight that did way more than levitate stuff.

I headed to the office, through the airlocks, back into the cool, where I flipped open the note. It said simply:

SS—
I hope I make it to you alive, but that ain't looking likely. I was ambushed. Shot. Made it to the Tesla and crawled through into the

hatch. Name of the shooter was One-Eyed Jack. They know about you. They're coming.
—BH

SS was me, Shining Smith. BH was Buck Harlan. *They* were the people who had killed him. And were coming for me.

"Coulda used a little more info in your note, Buck. But I'm sorry you died delivering it." Tears evaporated so fast I hardly noticed them gather.

I opened the small hatch of the armor niche and stepped up on the mounting pedestal. I was about to turn my back to the armor suit and initiate auto-donning when it occurred to me that appearing in military armor and weaponed up was acting out of fear and giving away my hand. It was one person heading in. Not an army. Maybe I was wrong that this person was coming for me. Maybe Harlan was wrong. Maybe my life as I knew it wasn't over.

If whoever sent Harlan to me, dead and all, had just wanted to kill me, I'd already be dead. If the military had figured out who I was, and half of what Smith's Junk and Scrap really was, my small part of the Earth would have been inundated with uniformed warriors. If the Gov. itself had found me, and knew what I was, the bureaucracy would have been more direct. A missile barrage would have arced over the junkyard and taken out everything, leaving nothing but a hole in the rock. End of Shining Smith.

So, I didn't need to wade in fighting. Yet.

Fear receded now that I was thinking and not just reacting. This wasn't done by any usual suspect who wanted me dead. No. Someone was sending me a message and a threat. Someone wanted something I was or something I had. I thought about the crashed spaceship debris half-buried out back, hidden beneath the best ghillie tech camo cloth ever devised. But no one knew about it, except for Mateo. And only Mateo knew the full nature of my defenses. So, they must be after the conventional weapons I had stockpiled for the eventual resurgence of the war.

I wasn't giving up my weapons, my money, or my ship. I especially wasn't giving up the weapons to traitors. And I sure as *hell* wasn't giving up my office.

I needed to go in with a presumptive position of weakness and lie through my teeth—assuming that, just because a motorcycle was heading this way, it was not my past nightmares come calling. It might not be. It could be coincidence.

I cursed and stepped away from the niche, into the personal toilette compartment—which would have been a bathroom if we had sufficient fresh water—and checked the lipstick. Combed my hair, which was still wet and spiked with sweat. Smeared on Kajal, desert-dweller's heavy eyeliner. Lips and lids were all the makeup the heat could stand. Anything more would melt off my face. I pulled the desert camo tank top and military cargo pants off my body and hung them to dry. Ran the body wand over my pits and privates. Spritzed on something to counteract my natural stink. Some women smelled of lilacs and roses. I'd been brought up a warrior. I dismantled vehicles and ran a black-market weapons business at a junkyard. To smell better would deny what I really was, and also, I just hated the stink of perfumes. I sprayed an extra layer of sunscreen over my very bronzed skin, because you can never have too much sunscreen, not since the WIMP explosion over Germany tore through the planet's electromagnetic shield and ripped all the good stuff out of the atmosphere.

"Location of bike?" I asked Mateo.

"Six klicks out. ARVAC cameras reveal male body shape, full face helmet, and cold-clothes, all in white and desert camouflage patterns. Bike is matte black."

His recon briefing paused. "Correction. Visual shielding has been activated. Bike is now desert patterns. Activating Silent Tracking."

Silent Tracking was something left to me by my father. At the time, it was the very latest in military R&D, a way to track most anything that created a visual, audible, or thermal trail even through the military's own shielding. Pops wasn't supposed to have that kind of tech, and I had no idea how he got it; I had no idea how he got *any* of the stuff I'd found here. The Silent Tracking had been stored in a kiosk in the middle of the junkyard when I returned, half dead and with a stolen, deranged warbot in tow. Then, I had discovered the other devices—the weapons systems, the AntiGravity Grabber—a stockpile of illegal weapons to which I had added significantly. The USSS *Sun-Star*—a spaceship built by the western alliance, led by the US—had crash-landed at some point prior to my arrival.

And then there was the office. The main reason I remained here, in a junkyard Pops had kept off the books, was the office.

And then the meaning of what Mateo had said hit home. Visual shielding on the bike meant military connections or a wannabe soldier. Either way it meant trouble.

"Calculation of burn time in the Tesla?" I asked Mateo.

"Two hours and sixteen minutes to clean bone. Four hours additional, give or take, to full ash."

Cremation would have taken about one hour. Maltodine was just as effective but it took longer. Six and a half hours. The sun would be down by then and the solar panels offline. I didn't have the battery power to run the Grabber into the night. I'd have to set the Tesla down soon and let it burn on the ground. But not while I had company.

"Speed of approaching vehicle is increasing. Suspect our ARVACs have been made."

"Fine. Bring them home and dock 'em. You geared up?"

"Little Girl, I'm always geared up."

Which was true. Mateo was semi-permanently attached to his bot. If he left it, if he was disconnected, he'd be dead inside a week. And he'd die badly. I'd seen him out of the suit when I placed him into the med-bay the week we met. It hadn't been a pretty sight.

At the closet, I ignored the dresses, which would not fit with the persona I was envisioning, and pulled on a bright pink tank, the color I chose surely inspired by the hot-pink of the AGR's paint job. The color made me look sweet and defenseless. Not like me at all. The tank and the matching cargo pants had belonged to Little Mama, my mother. They still smelled like her, and though it had been years since she died, tears threatened. Little Mama had looked cute when she rode bitch-seat on Pop's bike. But she had manned the guns for him when the war started, and had gone down fighting when the soldiers of the People's Republic of China's Central Military Commission landed in Port Angeles, Washington, with the first warbots. The Outlaws had been mid-rally when the PRC warbots walked ashore, and the motorcycle club had defended the public until the nearby cities had been evacuated.

That was the start of World War III and the end of the world as I had known it.

I was hell and gone from the war, I reminded myself. Hell and gone. But my nerves buzzed with adrenaline and fear as I slid a sweat-wicking, UV-protected, sheer dupatta over my tank. It wasn't cold clothes, but the dupatta fit the persona I was adopting. A civilian, a transplanted city girl who still looked to fashion. Dark tanned from sun exposure under the thinned atmosphere, weird eyes hidden under the 2-Gens, a stray lighter streak in my short, spiked hair from too much sun exposure. The grease under my nails and the chipped polish told the truth about me, and I probably should have repainted them, not that there was time.

No female ever went unarmed in the wild, so guns were okay even with the outfit. Under the dupatta I slung a harness around my shoulders and hips, and tightened it on my waist. Considered pulse weapons, but a scrapyard employee would more likely have explosive-based weaponry, not high-end military stuff. I checked the three 9-millimeter weapons the harness was built to hold, reconsidered, and clicked just one into place in its hemp-plaz holster. Added extra mags into the pockets. Basic minimal wear for a female employee in the wilds, like I was now pretending to be. I pulled on a pair of gloves to protect my fake persona and to protect the visitor from me, just in case he got close enough to touch.

"ARVAC data reveals the bike is a new variation of the OMW One Rider," Mateo said.

My hands froze. I stopped moving entirely.

"Silent Tracking scans reveal the One Rider has been militarized with after-stock equipment and weapons. Listing: One 9-millimeter Heckler & Koch MP8 UMP. Two 9-millimeter Heckler & Koch MP8 machine pistols. Two semiautomatic weapons on his person, make unknown. Though it's currently offline, the bike is equipped with a camouflaged miniaturized pulse weapon."

Bloody hell.

He was equipped to start a small war and half the bike stuff made no sense. Miniaturized pulse weapons were practically unknown outside of the military, and it was just weird on a Harley. The burning Tesla had been retrofitted with pulse weapons, based on dark matter, for battles in space, but no one—even Outlaw Militia Warriors—had access to it in peacetime. Unless the bike had been part of a government contract. OMW always had government contracts.

"Bugger," I cursed.

"The Harley has defensive shields available but not activated," Mateo said. "Bike's visual shielding is good. Maybe as good as mine." He hesitated. "Maybe better."

Mateo's military bot shielding was the very latest design from the end of the war. No one should have defensive or visual shielding as good as his. All the details meant that the dude riding up to my place of business and arriving just after Harlan's untimely demise and appearance wasn't a fluke or coincidence. Whoever the traitors to the war effort were, they had found me. Unless . . . Unless I'd been found by more than one group or person, because worst-case scenarios were just my dumb luck.

If so, then one group had killed Harlan. Another had sent a rep carrying a Universal Machine Pistol and the latest in OMW weapons. Within minutes of each other? A different kind of message or the OMW responding to the first message?

Bloody damn.

I could kill the rider. I could toss him in with Harlan, whose body was currently powering the Maltodine burn. But my newest visitor was surely tracked and others would come.

In his wonderful British accent, Pops had once said to the OMWs, "The world is changing, lads. We have to adapt. We have to evolve. To remain static is death."

"Pops," I had said from the front row, where I was watching his speech. "Even corpses change." I knew. I'd seen enough of them.

Some of the warriors had laughed. Pops hadn't.

And then Little Mama had died. And I had been swarmed by bicolors. And we had done the unthinkable, a lot of unthinkables. And Pops had started dying, slow bit by slow bit as the Parkinson's ate his body and his brain. I had tried but been unable to save him. Nothing had saved him.

I slammed my feet into cute, heeled boots and ran a finger up the seal. Crammed a clean hat, with a wide brim and a faded silk rose, on my head. I snatched a nail file out of the flowerpot that had once held Little Mama's orchids, wiped two insulated bottle keepers, and plucked two iced drinks out of the fridge, wiping them as I raced out of the office through the first and then the second airlock doors. Sealing both airlock doors on the cold air inside, I walked out to meet the rider. The heat hit me like a wrecking ball and fresh sweat broke out all over.

"Activating perimeter defenses," Mateo said.

"You never deactivate them," I said.

"True," he said. "But the road along our front border and the drive stay at DEFCON four unless we expect trouble. Now we're at DEFCON three."

"Why DEFCON three?"

"Because something smells."

Since Mateo no longer had a real nose, I knew he meant figuratively.

"You aren't armored up," he stated.

"I'm going for Little Mama's defensive tactics," I said, setting the icy bottles in their holders in the shade, not that the shade offered much protection from the summer heat.

"Ahhh. Poor guy." It wasn't easy to tell, but Mateo sounded almost happy about the coming carnage. "ETA sixty seconds."

I knew that by the sound of the bike. There were muters on the engine, the soft snore familiar for a wartime One Rider Harley in infiltrator mode. I missed the full-throated war-bike roar, the wind in my hair, the road thrumming through my body. I missed that freedom.

I pulled a chair into the shade of the AG Grabber; the seat was padded and so hot from the scalding sun that it burned my butt through the cloth of Mama's pink pants, but there wasn't time to cool the seat or baby my butt. I slid the converted, inverted shooting table in front of me and I propped my booted feet on it. Unlatching the thumb-lock on the table, I made sure it would invert in its usual half second if I dropped my feet, exposing the prewar M249 Para Gen II Belt-Fed Machine Gun, currently mounted on the table's other side. The weapon was hidden by the heavy-duty, honeycombed composite sheeting that was actually a pretty good shield for most small arms fire. I had repurposed it from mid-grade-quality space scrap. If an enemy assassin riding a bike had found me, there wouldn't be enough left of him or his bike to send home in a box.

The burn inside the Tesla had superheated the desert hot-as-the-entrance-to-hell air. Sweat was trickling down my spine.

If the OMW had found me, I didn't know what would happen. I was supposed to be dead. If two groups had found me . . . I was well and truly screwed.

The muted engine noise grew closer and changed trajectory as it slowed and turned down the drive.

"Company's here," Mateo said. "All systems go."

Sweat slid between my boobs and soaked into my clothes across my back and belly. The sun beat down around me like nuclear fallout, forty-five degrees C in the shade. Water boiled at a hundred, so I was half-way to scalded. I popped the top of one drink and took a long pull, set it aside, pulled off one glove, and flipped the nail file up. I was as ready as I was going to get. The bike went silent. I gave it a good five-second pause before I called out, "I've got a cold drink with your name on it if you come with cash to buy."

Five more seconds went by as the rider either got into a better position to kill me or tried to decide how to proceed. Mateo didn't update me, so I was betting my death wasn't intended. Yet.

Another five seconds went by. And another.

I caught a slight reflection as Mateo moved into place between the entrance and me, his seven-and-a-half-meter tall warbot suit in full visual shielding, his head invisible behind a meter of horizontal silk-plaz view screen.

Mateo muttered, "Body posture is too ready."

I relaxed just a bit. Filed a rough spot off my trigger fingernail. The black engine grease around my cuticle was a dead giveaway that I wasn't the girly girl the clothes suggested. If I let the stranger get close enough to see that grime, I better already know he wasn't a threat.

I really needed to give myself a full mani.

From the corner of my eye, I caught a flash of movement. A big solid-gray cat was crouched on the roof of the office, one of the two breeding males of the prides of junkyard cats. His fighting partner, a black-haired, green-eyed male devil, raced along a branched, prewar electrical pole leaning against an old earth-mover. Dang cats had heard the sound of the bike and come to investigate. I tried to remember the last time I had provided the junkyard cats a ritual offering—dead goat or cave bat—and nothing came to mind. The most I'd had to share lately was my water and some goat milk. Nothing high in protein. I hoped they'd behave, but they were cats, so it wasn't likely.

"He's changing gear. Still armed," Mateo murmured into my earbud. "Lighting a cigar."

That was a good sign. I couldn't see an assassin

taking time to start a smoke.

The two male cats inched closer to the edges of their perches. As one, the hunting females raised heads and looked over the open space I currently occupied, then back to the entrance, before hiding again. I had no idea what they were looking at, but the prides were synchronized enough to be scary; it reminded me of the bicolors and their modifications. Reminded me again that I had made mistakes over the years. Big ones.

My visitor walked around the corner. Two meters tall, with a strong neck and broad sloping shoulders, a chest like a brick shithouse, narrow waist, and huge hands, each finger wearing a ring, like disconnected knucks. Fast-looking and rangy, if rangy was also big enough to play offensive tackle in the NFL. *Bugger was big.* Sweaty brown hair was cut two centimeters long and lay flat to his skull, his beard a half centimeter of buzz. Brown skin, maybe Hispanic, maybe American tribal, maybe mixed Cauc and Surprise Special, like me. Little Mama hadn't known her ethnic heritage and Pops hadn't cared. My visitor's brown eyes were hard and focused on me. He was neither happy nor unhappy. A smart, violent man with a job he liked and was scary good at.

He must have left the protective gear on the bike, because he wore battle boots, no cold coat or pants, no sunglasses or helmet, just brownish Harley Davidson riding plex and a loose, long-sleeved T-shirt in desert camo. Over his shirt, he wore an OMW kutte, the official riding vest of the Outlaws, and though I had mostly expected it, my body went into battle stillness.

The leather vest was worn and raw in places, and was fully covered with chapter patches from a whole bunch of the pre-war states. More significant were the patches from post-war foreign countries. He had traveled the world for the Outlaws even after the peace treaty. This asshole was a *very important dude* in the OMW. He had been called to serve *every*where.

Maybe most important, he had a patch from the mother chapter in old Chicago. *Criminy*. Whoever he was, he was more than a full patch member, more than just a made-man. His patches showed he had moved up in the world from a nobody to a national sergeant-at-arms—also known as an enforcer—which meant he reported to the vice president of the entire club. The club motto patch—"God Forgives, Outlaws Don't, ADIOS"—was worn and . . . maybe blood-splattered. In this day when any drop of blood could instantly ID the donor, that was brave. Or scary stupid. Or proud of the death of his enemies. I went with door number three. There was a dark bulge at his belt, a handgun, butt exposed—a big-mother semi-automatic. The grip was marked with a scarlet skull and crossbones. The biometric marker indicated it was linked to him alone. An expensive, high-tech, killer's gun. Assassins used them when they wanted to make a statement.

"Bugger," I muttered aloud to Mateo.

"Not interested," the visitor said with an easy smile. He stopped in the shade of the office, his head nearly touching the overhang and directly under the gray cat. He stood hipshot and puffed on the cigar. The smell of the smoke and the sight of the kutte reminded me of Pops, and I narrowed my eyes against tears. I couldn't afford an emotional reaction now. I sipped, waiting for the moisture to dry out in the heat.

He puffed several times. Clenched the cigar in his teeth. Smoke curling up but missing his eyes.

"You say you got a cold one?"

His voice was low and gravely. And his mouth did interesting things around the cigar. If I needed to goad him, I could. He looked like the kind of man who'd be

irritated at being accused of getting friendly with another man, and his reaction to the word *bugger* confirmed it.

"If you're here to waste my time, no. If you're a
paying customer, cash only, I got beer. Stout." I
flashed a now-smooth fingernail at the beers. "Bottle's been out of the cold for two minutes, but in a
holder, in the shade. It's still drinkable." I didn't hold
up the bottle, but I did place a finger on the flip table's
release button.

He didn't move.

"I might be buying. You the boss?"

"It's his day off. I'm Smith's Junk and Scrap's receptionist and accountant. I can make any deal he can
make. Maybe better."

"Why better?"

"Because I know what bills are due tomorrow. He
never looks and wouldn't care if he did."

The two fighter cats turned in unison and stared
at me, right where my finger was perched on the release button. That meant there was a female directly
behind me, watching and transmitting the info to all
the other cats. The cats had mad mental skills and
they communicated by scent or body language or
fricking ESP for all I knew. My neck crawled with near
panic. I didn't like a hungry pride cat behind me. I'd
seen them scavenge for protein. It was not pretty.

The Outlaw puffed. Smoke blew out and dissipat-
ed. The silence went on too long, as if this was a test.
The hairs on my nape lifted despite the sweat and I
felt almost cold. Nerves scuttled along my skin like
bicolor ants, and my wrist burned, wanting to be used.
But he was too far away, thankfully. My heart rate
sped. And I blew it.

"You got a handle I can use? Or is Enforcer good
enough?"

The man went still as a bot.

Bloody damn. I'd just proved I knew what he was. I lied fast, part truth, part fabrication.

"My mama used to date an Outlaw. He got his teeth knocked out by an enforcer. He deserved it. I never forgot the patch."

The man waited. Considering. Sucked on the cigar. Smoke curled. It was harsh, stronger than the burned Maltodine stink.

"What'd he do?" he asked at last. "The man your mama dated."

"He was using cocaine. He beat Mama. He tried to beat me. I hid. Then the enforcer came. We never had that problem again."

"His handle?"

"Darson. Or as I called him, and all bikers since, Asshole."

He considered, his eyes tightening as he pulled the name up from a memory Berger-chip. Darson had been given an attitude adjustment when I was ten or eleven. I'd witnessed it. It had been bloody, but the reports said he went through voluntary withdrawal, never used again, and he stopped beating up his old lady and her daughter. They had all been killed in Seattle at the first of the war, right after the Chinese landed. Or, like a lot of records, their reported deaths might have been wrong.

"I'm Jagger."

"Good name for a pit bull. Gold gets you the best pricing, but cash is good too. What are you buying?"

He didn't react to being called a dog. "I got cash." Which said nothing about whether or what he was buying, but my persona would have accepted that.

"You want that beer while it's cold, you can come over."

"What's on the other side of the table?" he asked instead.

I glanced down at my lap. "I'd have expected a

better come on from a pit bull named Jagger."

He smiled. I smiled. He went for the handgun. I flipped the table, ducked, and aimed. He was fast, but he was human, and I wasn't where I'd been. He was looking down the barrel of the M249 Para Gen II Belt-Fed Machine Gun. The gun's retrofit auto sights and war-time firing mechanism were trained on him. I had a good forty-six centimeters of ammo ready to go.

Meanwhile, I was now protected by a flap of material constructed from part of a space-capable warship. I was effectively shielded from anything he might be carrying. Lucky, that. Because he was holding a 40-caliber H&K, a mid-war weapon created for close-in work against the Russian bloc in Eastern Europe. I'd been right. A blow-'em-to-hell-and-back, down-and-dirty, leave-a-message-splattered-on-the-walls weapon.

"Nice," he said. Outlaws might use pulse weapons in wartime, but they were all gun nuts at heart. And the Para Gen was a made-man's fantasy gun.

The motion revealing the haft of a knife in a hip sheath, he put away the down-and-dirty gun. I didn't put away the Para Gen. He walked over, watching as the barrel followed him. He chuckled as if having an auto-targeting system and enough ammo to rip apart an elephant was amusing. He stopped in front of the barrel, and it was pointed at his solar plexus. I returned to my chair, feet up like before. Shoved the extra beer across to him with my boot. It slid with a smooth sound, leaving behind a trail of water. The stouts had been on a separate table leaf and hadn't flown into the desert air. I'd never waste good beer.

I drank down half of mine. He looked over my weapons as he popped the top and drank his. Stopped. Lowered the bottle. Studied me. His eyes changed. The lie had been perfect. But that was when I knew I'd screwed up. I just didn't know how bad.

He blew a smoke ring. I didn't care much for most tobacco, but good quality cigars were an exception. The smoke and the scent fit him. Something like longing filled me. Longing was dangerous. My wrist itched. I narrowed my eyes at him. Not that he could tell much behind my orange lenses.

He tapped ash. Talked around the cigar. "I'm looking for a kutte."

Holy hell.

"Oh?"

"Special kutte. Been missing a while. Tracking sensor was activated a week ago."

I had admitting to knowing about Outlaw Militia Warriors, so I couldn't say I didn't know what he was talking about. Pops' OMW kutte was in the vault, vacuum-sealed. I hadn't touched it. No one had. Not even air had touched it. No way it had been activated.

If Harlan had been decomposing in *his* kutte, it was a goner and I was screwed. OMWs didn't burn kuttes except at a proper ceremony.

However. Pops' kutte wasn't the only one on site.

I set my mouth as if I was thinking through inventory; I figured it out fast. My kutte was hanging in my wardrobe. It had a few ancient wartime sensors implanted in the patches, warnings about fumes from gas-attacks, a radiation sensor, that sort of thing. All of them had gone offline years ago as the batteries finally died. But there was one particular sensor, one I hadn't thought about in years, that had been put together by Pops just before he passed, after I'd been swarmed by bicolors and after I'd had my run-in with a Mama-Bot, but before I'd had to run. If its battery had survived the war and the years . . .

I blinked behind my sunglasses and took a slow breath of dry desert air.

"Triggered a week ago? What triggers it?" I asked, as fear began to glide across my shoulders and down my spine. Because I already knew.

"PRC warriors or bots," Jagger said casually. Too casually. His eyes watching me intently.

Since there were no more warriors from the People's Republic of China left alive this far east, that meant an autobot was nearby.

A PRC warbot was on my land. A *Perker*. Its presence had triggered the sensor and notified the mother chapter I was in trouble.

I came slowly upright. Dropped my feet.

As Mateo processed the same things I had, he cursed into my earbud, softly, long, and inventively. His voice carried anger, as much as his metallic voice allowed. Mateo hated Perkers and with good reason.

I looked at the hunter cats. They were no longer looking at me. Or the OMW. They were tracking something. Cat heads swung back and forth as they accumulated info and stored it in their linked consciousness. Something besides the enforcer was on the property.

Bloody damn hell.

In my peripheral vision, I tracked the cats as I put it all together.

Each PRC warbot—*Perkers* in the lingo—was unique, created by the massive things the U.S. military called Mama-Bots. They were built according to a bot algorithm only another bot could understand. The PRC Mama-Bots had pulled themselves out of the waters of Possession Sound, Washington, and begun destroying everything in their paths. With the detritus of destroyed cities, their mechanical nanobots built Perker Crawlers. The Crawlers crawled off the Mama-Bot assembly lines by the thousands and hitched a ride on anything that moved, crossing the country, moving east until they found a place that looked nice, a town or small city, which they destroyed and took apart to make more of themselves. Or, they buried themselves in the soil like mines, hidden where they could stay for years.

Each Crawler had a timer or trigger that set it off. When activated, they'd dig themselves out of the soil, like locusts or cicadas, and go hunting. Find a target. Destroy it. Perker Crawlers could be the size of a tank or as small as a wheelbarrow, but none had been seen in the West Virginia desert in more than five years, mostly because there was only stone near about, no soil to bury themselves in. Also, they had to travel to get here, and *here* was the middle of freaking nowhere. Crawler AIs were smart. They went to cities where they could cause mega-damage, not into a desert of stone.

Unless one had been targeted at me, or deliberately dropped off near here, and something had triggered it to come hunting me. And the Perker then set off the kutte. The fear-sweat trickling down my spine went cold in the heat.

"A week ago," I clarified softly, "you say the sensor you're looking for was triggered. By a Perker."

A *week ago* a Perker had entered my land. My kutte had sent out an alarm to OMW central. Yet Mateo and I and our exquisite security system hadn't received the alarm or spotted the Perker. Because we hadn't been looking. We'd gotten sloppy.

Bloody damn, bloody damn, bloody damn!

In my earbud, Mateo suggested a sexual activity that was anatomically impossible by anything with bones. I rolled to my feet, slamming my ungloved hand into the war-sleeve at my side. It clamped around my hand, forearm, and molded to fit up to my bicep, the scales adjusting to my slender form instead of the muscular dead soldier I'd taken it from. Moving faster and smoother than pure-human. Way faster. I aimed my weapon at my assassin, and a piercing green laser centered on his chest with a soft hum and latched on.

He tensed all over at the transformation in my body language and position. And my speed. And the fact that I was now wearing a functioning section of military Dragon Scale exoskeleton anti-recoil armor, a war-sleeve with a Smith & Wesson XVR 460 Magnum now poking out the end. His expression said he recognized that the S&W's auto targeting system had acquired the target. And the target was him. Which was way more impressive to warriors than the big, in-your-face Para Gen.

My visitor was a dead man smoking. Double dead. The two weapons trained on him would churn him to hamburger. The Asshole puffed, squinted, and grinned.

"Defenses," I said to Mateo, now not caring that Jagger heard. "Anything?"

"Nothing followed him. Scanning vids and stills from perimeter cams. Searching everything from the past week."

"We got problems," I said to the OMW enforcer as the female hunter cats leaped or belly-crawled to join the fighter cats. They were in two groups, staring in two directions. We had *two* Perkers? "You know how to fight, Jagger?"

"Happy to make your acquaintance," he said, relaxed, still amused. "But you have me at a disadvantage."

He puffed. A perfect smoke ring left his mouth.

A disadvantage? Oh. I knew his name. I hadn't given mine.

"I asked you a question," I half-growled.

"I do okay. I survived the Battle of Mobile."

Mateo laughed harder than I'd ever heard him. It would have been a belly laugh, if he had a belly. Anyone who survived the Battle of Mobile with all his limbs and his mind intact was a miracle man with the luck of the Irish.

"I like this guy," Mateo said. "Ask if he's ready to rumble."

His breathing had sped up. Mateo was getting ready to go to war.

"Update," I demanded of him.

Jagger's eyes narrowed. He flicked them everywhere, seeking out the location of my confidant. Or his war-time instincts had finally gone on alert.

Mateo said, "I got nothing. Nothing on scans, but the cats' body language says we have more than one Perker. Behind the Outlaw and behind you. Attempting to pinpoint positions."

Behind my glasses, my eyes darted, searching, seeing nothing. My body tensed to make the rush to the airlock door and the armored-and-weaponized office. But between my position and the office there was a wide-open space, no cover, and Jagger.

Mateo needed to detect the Perker Crawler, or Crawlers, before I moved. To Mateo I said, "Do a stills comparison. Look for something that didn't get caught by the perimeter motion sensors, moving too slow for the monitors, a Crawler, something that's in a different place every time an auto shot is taken." The sensors were set to go off if anything moved more than two centimeters an hour. The security system took pics every fifteen minutes no matter what.

Jagger's body didn't change, but his eyes narrowed as he took in my demand about a Crawler warbot.

"Anybody can *survive*," I said to Jagger, pushing him, needing to push something, fight someone, my body flooding with chemicals and adrenaline. "You know how to *fight*, Asshole?"

"I was born fightin'."

"Yeah? You fight many Crawlers when you were wearing diapers?"

"No sign of Crawlers," Mateo said, "no sign of entry point."

Asshole puffed once more, but he didn't look so amused or relaxed now. "I've taken on a Perker Crawler. It's been a good five years since I saw a slow-bot."

The Mama-Bot Perkers had made thousands of Crawlers. No way had they all been destroyed.

"Same for me," I said. "Crawlers don't have good hiding space here."

"No soil," he agreed. "You got mine cracks. Makes it hard for them to travel." Mine cracks were deep narrow drops into the earth, formed by the caving-in of old underground mines or by mountaintop removal. "Arsenic, toxic coal dust, benzene, and carbon monoxide never stopped a Perker Crawler, though," he said.

Mateo cursed.

The fact that Jagger knew the terminology and the chemicals in the local earth made my insides clench. Asshole knew too much that was info only a local would know. Or he had a better Berger-chip silicone implant than I'd ever heard of and had accessed local info.

"Update," I demanded of Mateo, panic setting in. The cats' body language said this was taking too long.

"Still no visual confirmation of Perker Crawlers."

I had never seen this OMW before. If Jagger *was* an OMW. But what if he was someone else? A plant. He was still targeted. If he moved, he was dead. But we didn't have much time. Not if we had a Crawler on the property. The cats looked back and forth. Two Crawlers. Yeah. *Bugger.*

"Who's prez now?" I asked.

Asshole's eyes narrowed.

"I've got a video trail," Mateo said, grim as rust. "Medium-small Crawler. Still shots show it approached the border two weeks ago moving less than two-point-five centimeters an hour. Once over the border, it sped up. According to current readings, your asshole's right. Your jacket sent out an alert seven days ago, and it's still pulsing."

Unless I could spin this, and Jagger bought my story and went away peaceably, the Outlaws would know who I was and where I was. And it was possible that Jagger had been doing high-altitude ARVAC flyovers. I had defenses against Auto Remote Viewing Air Craft, but I kept their notification sensors turned down. With all the raptors around, eating toxic rats and bats that crawled and flew out of the mine cracks, I had set the parameters low. Too low.

Bloody damn.

"And Shining," Mateo said in my ear. "I messed up. Bad. The crawler found the *SunStar*. The slow-bot released one of the *SunStar*'s hatches and stayed inside for nearly seventy-two hours. When it came out, there were two of them with more cumulative mass than when they went in. I'm running ship internal scans. Eventually, I'll figure out what the Crawler plundered through and stole, but for now, the slow-bots have augmented themselves with space-going tech or shielding. And they're both missing."

Which meant the Perker Crawler had started out as a single slow-bot, stolen space-going equipment, and its mech-nanos had reconfigured it, breaking down into two smaller Crawlers before it came hunting me. *Two.*

I looked at the cats. They were slinking back, but still watching two different locations. *Bloody damn.* It—*they*—had found the office. Perkers were here. Targeting me. Flop sweat trickling down my spine turned to ice. I could shoot Jagger and get inside alone but if he was OMW they would send backup, and no one who took out an enforcer lived to tell the tale.

Also, a second fighter might be handy short term. If he was who he said he was.

"Who's prez now?" I repeated to Jagger, flexing the Dragon Scale armor as a threat, my voice taking on tension as I calculated all my odds. "And who do you report to?"

"Faria. I report to McQuestion."

I chuckled. The command structure of the OMWs had shifted, but only high-level made-men knew it. The prez of the Outlaws used to be important, back before the war. Now he was the PR head, the one the cops and the media *thought* was the top dog, while the man with the real power was the vice-president, and his name was never given. The VP was always referred to as McQuestion. Asshole had just proven himself the real deal, or as close as I could get without scanning him and his tattoos with a viber, which would mean him taking off his clothes.

In my peripheral vision, a cat leaped into the air. Others did the same. I tensed, not knowing why they—

Gunfire rang out over the junkyard.

Asshole leaped toward the office, drawing his weapon, dropping to the earth. Wartime reflexes.

Mateo cursed.

I fell into a crouch, mostly hidden beneath the rotating table, and slid the Para Gen from auto-targeting to manual. I had forty-six centimeters of ammo. Not enough. Good thing I'd put the weapon sleeve on. I flipped a switch on my 2-Gen glasses and gave myself access to Mateo's screens. It was a dizzying array and had taken months for me to use the glasses without tossing my cookies, but now I could follow Mateo's tech vision.

Enemy rapid fire followed. Full auto. Short bursts. The third volley of shots raced across the front of the office, dinging and pinging and ricocheting away, not penetrating its armor. The Crawlers and my unwanted visitor probably now knew the office wasn't an ordinary building.

"Narrowing search patterns," Mateo said, sounding more contained now that battle had begun and his suit had injected him with 'roids and flooded his body with synth-pheromones.

The Crawlers fired again, destroying my fake satellite receivers. Plastic and bits of copper and old computer parts flew everywhere. I'd stuffed the fakes with parts to make someone think they had taken an outdated system offline. The EntNu stuff was inside the spaceship—where the Crawler had been. *Damn*. The Perkers fired, hitting my rain catcher on the roof. Not that it had rained in the last two years, but still.

Bastards.

Jagger sprinted, now behind a stack of old engine blocks ready for crushing. Smart move.

"Located," Mateo said. "Perker Bot-A is confirmed at fifteen meters from you at your two o'clock. Perker Bot-B is at your six, twelve meters and closing."

Like I'd thought. Behind me. *Bloody hell*.

Mateo's vid screens divided, showing two images, current date, and time. I watched as the matte-black half-bots trundled toward the office at full speed. The larger bot, Bot-A, moved three centimeters a minute. The smaller one, Bot-B, had fewer foldouts but was twice as fast. Bot-A had more weapons, Bot-B had speed.

On a third screen, I saw a dark hulking reflection moving in on three legs, lifting himself over ancient transmissions, rusting body parts, racks of hatches and doors, a century or so of vehicles, most of which were on-site long before the war. The warbot Mateo was on the move in stealth mode, his long legs rising and setting down, his three longest limbs providing balance like a spider's legs to facilitate both speed and silence. His warbot suit looked like an old kid's toy, only a lot more deadly.

"Can you get a shot?" I asked.

To my right, a cat—the gray male—leaped across a pathway, three meters in the air, and disappeared. A striped female skulked on the ground around a stack of disintegrating tires.

They were hunting the Crawlers? Why?

"Targets acquired. Take cover," Mateo instructed.

Shouting the instructions to Jagger, I curled into a fetal position behind the table, hands over my head. Not that the position would save me. If any size Perker Crawler got to me, even with the table shielding, it would take me apart. Perkers were patient, thorough, and nearly indestructible.

"Firing WaMAW." A *WaMAW* was a Warbot-Launched Multipurpose Assault Weapon. A big-ass shotgun, a small cannon, or a small missile launcher, based on the ammo used.

Mateo fired. Fired again. And again. Which seemed like so much overkill.

"Did you get it?" I shouted over the concussive damage to my ears.

"Negative. It's . . ." Mateo cursed again. "It's got ship shielding."

The Perker had gone into the *SunStar*. It had dismantled some part of the engine shielding, or maybe the shielding off a midsized space-going observation capsule, and adapted it to its own exoskeleton. I needed to get inside the office. But I'd have to cross the space between my dubious protection and the doorway, which they had likely been waiting on all along. And Jagger was now nowhere in sight.

I took a breath that stank of the remembered reek of war-sweat and burned ammo. I forced my body to uncurl. Carefully, knowing what I was about to say might set Mateo off, I asked, "Do the Crawlers have Puffers?" A Perker Crawler often carried Puffers. Puffers carried mechanical nanobots. Puffer mech-nanos had taken Mateo down.

Mateo hissed out a breath, metallic and grinding and full of fury. "Searching."

Puffers were attendant, automatic, weaponized mini-bots that could slide out of the Perkers' receptacles and go hunting on their own. Mini-recon-bots, or hand grenades on wheels, or specialized cutting and dismembering systems on wheels, all with versatile, origami-inspired construction, allowing the wheels to collapse inward, and the mini-bot to fold into a flat configuration, like a horseshoe crab. NASA had invented them for Mars explorers. Mama-Bots had stolen the concept and weaponized the Puffers. Puffers swarmed like bicolor ants, and because they were solar powered, and had mech-nanotech self-healing, self-altering, Puffer-building capabilities, they simply never, ever stopped. They had to be crushed or pried open one by one and blasted with AntiGrav to kill them.

Unless someone had a secret weapon.

Or *was* a secret weapon.

"Let me know when you see them."

"You can't," Mateo snarled. "You don't even know if it will work."

"If I don't try, they'll kill us eventually. The only way you fought the nanobots inside your suit was to close it down, set it to run on auto, and hunt them one at a time. And that was in a confined space where they couldn't run and hide and reproduce and come back with more bots. It took months and you nearly died. Out here we'll lose for sure."

They were bad, horrible months. The nanos had been inside his suit a long time before they had reproduced enough to start making changes to the suit. And they had eaten parts of him before he figured out that AntiGrav forces would destroy nanos. We'd had to blast his entire suit.

"We have an *entire junkyard* for them to hide in," I said, trying to convince him.

"You have a witness. You can*not*."

I thought about Buck Harlan in the Tesla. He died getting me a message, probably the message that the Perker Crawler was on the way—a death sentence. The Perker now knew I had a spaceship on the property, which would motivate it even more to destroy me. And the Asshole? He was a black hole of uncertain possibilities, none of them good.

Someone knew I was here. But that someone didn't know what I could do.

"Shining. We don't even know if it will work. Try it my way first." Mateo stopped, fired. When the dust started to settle and I hadn't answered, he added, "Please." Mateo didn't beg. Not ever. About anything.

His polite request was a first and it made me melt inside—an angry melt, but still a melt.

"*Fine*," I snarled. "According to the screens, Bot-A is nearly in position to take me. Bot-B has stopped and is waiting for A to achieve attack position. Concur?"

"Concur. I'm in position with a clear line of fire to both. On *three* I'll lay down attack and cover fire and you get into the office. If you see Jagger, take him with you."

"You sure about him?"

"Hell, no. But he's human and he's OMW. We don't leave either to a Perker. *One*."

My body went liquid, as battle chemicals and human adrenalin flushed into my bloodstream like a flash flood. Still wearing the Dragon Scale armor sleeve, I slammed the Para Gen to full auto and swiped control of the weapon to Mateo.

"*Two*."

Crouching, I braced my feet. Placed the palm of

the war-sleeve on the AG Grabber support.

"Three! Gogogogogogo."

I was already moving, shoving off, the Dragon scale sleeve stretching and contracting, throwing me across the wide-open space and through the air. Jarring my shoulder, spine, and pelvis, but making me freaking *move.*

Mateo fired, a double barrage of ammo. I went deaf. My feet touched down in the dirt three-and-a-half meters from my previous perch. Legs bent. Thrusted into a dead sprint. Battle reflexes, honed and augmented by what I'd become.

The Crawler bots fired. Blasted the air where I'd been and the front of the office. But I was inside the protective airlock. Heaving myself inside. Faster than pure human.

"Where's Jagger?" I shouted over the sound of gunfire and the airlocks closing.

"Searching."

"Screens!" I said into the odd silence, slapping a headset on and slamming my body into the over-sized defensive Neuro-Based-Pressure command seat designed for space travel. The Dragon Scale war-sleeve slipped into the control unit and connected. Every screen in the junkyard came online. On three of them, I saw cats fighting with Puffers. *Bloody hell. Puffers.* On one screen, two striped females were a ball of fur, fangs, and claws against tech. The gray fighter male was rolling across the dirt with another Puffer. A third mini-bot was disassembled next to the body of its cat attacker.

That thing killed my cat!

"Where are they?" I snarled. Bot-A and Bot-B had disappeared. Except for the cats, patrolling in stalking groups of three or four, nothing moved.

Using remote activation, I dropped the hot-as-a-furnace AGR Tesla with a *whomp* I felt through my feet, and redirected the AG Grabber, wishing I had a portable model. The Grabber arm swung clockwise. I had to blast the injured Puffers before their AIs ordered their nanos to rebuild. Mateo's painful experience suggested I had around two minutes before the reconstruction of the broken Puffers commenced.

"Jagger is behind the office," Mateo said. "Four meters from the back hatch."

I flipped switches and brought up the rear screens. Jagger was holding a bleeding cat in the curve of one elbow and his weapon in the other hand. The cigar was nowhere to be seen.

"Is he clear?"

"Affirmative."

I engaged the back airlock to prepare to open and flashed the green light above it three times. Then three more times. It caught Jagger's eyes and he nodded, knowing—hoping?—he was on camera. I flashed the light once. Waited a beat, flashed it a second time. Waited a beat. Giving him a rhythm. Something flew through the air from behind Jagger. The office array sights identified it as a spinning fragmentary grenade. The war-sleeve targeted the frag and fired. A small laser drilled across the spinning surface and through the small bomb. Still four meters out, it exploded.

Jagger ducked.

The green light flashed again. The airlock hatch popped open.

Jagger sprinted and dove into the airlock. I closed the outer hatch and took out another mini-grenade launcher. Spotted the Puffers that had fired them, both rolling beneath the fuselage of a Boeing-constructed warplane.

Damn.

I punched open the inner hatch, and Jagger rolled inside before it opened halfway and I punched it closed. I didn't look around. There wasn't time. With the war-sleeve, I lifted the AG Grabber over the closest downed Puffers out front and engaged the mechanism. It was hard to kill Puffers, but if you managed to rupture the exoskeleton and then hit it with AntiGrav, it fried the internal nanobots. Without the nanos, the Puffer wasn't coming back. The Puffers rose into the air and vibrated as the energies hit them.

Jagger settled to one knee. He was breathing hard, trying to blow off toxic adrenaline breakdown chemicals, but he still saw too much. "Where the hell did you get all this?" he asked, meaning the office, the launching systems that had rolled out to fire the weapons, the recoilless firing systems, the spaceworthy tech of the screens and command board. And the roomy, extra-extra-large NBP seat. The chair was clearly not designed for a human. But this was a scrap yard. Scrappers could get stuff others couldn't. At least that was what I hoped he might conclude.

So, I didn't reply, just aimed the AG Grabber at a half-dozen Puffers Mateo had crushed into pieces with a car engine. It sucked them all up at once. The Puffers did the AG dance as they expired, their little nano brains fried. I set them to cook and added a timer for the Grabber to auto shutdown.

"You're her, aren't you? Shining Smith?"

A frisson of shock and fear sliced through me. Bot-A emerged from the protection of a skid full of big prewar electric motors. I fired everything I had at it. The concussion of that much ammo juddered into the office and shook my body.

"No idea what you're talking about, Asshole. The two Puffers who fired the frags are still loose, I have two more Puffers that need to be fried, and"—my voice rose—"I'm low on ammo." I flicked a glance at him to make sure he knew I was ticked off and busy. "You up for loading or do I need to ask the Crawlers to take a break so I can hold your hand and sing 'Kumbaya?'"

Jagger laughed, the deep tones scraping along my spine.

"You got a mouth on you. I like it. I can load, but your cat is dying."

I spared the cat in his arms a glance. It was the gray male fighter cat. My heart sank at the same time it softened because a man carrying and caring for an injured cat was weirdly sweet. Remotely, I slapped the med-bay open. A soft pink light lit the room.

"Schedule C1 is for male cat."

Jagger rose to the med-bay and chuckled because I had a med-bay already programed for cats. I heard the appropriate clicks, followed by the *whoosh* and the hum as the med-bay engaged. As I scanned for the Crawlers, I heard the snapping as Jagger began loading ammo into the depleted office weapons and removed shells that had dropped into the capture nets. Without a pause he also loaded the heaver weaponry. Maybe he really had been at the Battle of Mobile. Everything was recognizable to him because the office's offensive and defenses arrays had been modified with Earth-based weapons. All the good stuff was hidden, though his questions about where I'd gotten all this stuff likely meant he was going to figure out way too much.

"Why aren't they dead yet?" he asked of the small Crawlers. "You've expended enough ammo to take down a tank."

Unless I could come up with a plausible lie, I'd have to tell him about the spaceship buried out back. *Bugger.* I rapid-fired three 9-millimeter hollow points at a Puffer. Shifted the AG Grabber to the downed Puffer and fried it. Sighted another Puffer and repeated the process, treating them to the AntiGrav energies as fast as I killed them.

Mateo said into my earbud, "Bot-A identified. It

has SS armor-piercing warheads and it's targeting the office."

I found the screen, ID'd the aisle number, and saw it was a straight shot to the office. SS armor-piercing warheads were designed to take out spaceship armor. The shrapnel alone could be sufficient to damage even the office. I had to risk powering up the office's defensive shields. They'd be visible from satellites and I'd be totally screwed if the Gov. found me, but screwed might be better than dead. The fact that it was still daylight and energies might be hard to detect from space convinced me. I ripped off my glove and slammed my left index finger down on the screen, activating the WIMP-particle-based shields. A faint orange glow filled the air, sparkling off the dust and weapon-fire smoke hanging there. Mateo fired. The blasts shook the raw stone under the office and up through the office floor. Jagger cursed in surprise.

"Bot-A down. Fry it," Mateo said.

I flipped off the shields, found the disabled bot on the screens, and swung the Grabber toward it. "It doesn't reach. And I'm blowing through my stored power like prewar Vegas. I can't keep this up."

"Recommendations?" Mateo asked, only a hint of snark in his voice.

"Can you pick up an engine block and use that to shove it six meters closer down Aisle Alpha One?"

"I might miss some pieces."

Which meant Puffers and nanos all over the junk-yard. I blinked away frustrated tears, thinking about hunting Puffers for months.

"We got no other options. Except to say we need a portable AG Grabber."

"Hindsight," he agreed, more gently. "You might be the brains to my brawn, but you aren't perfect."

No, I wasn't perfect. I knew that. But with Mateo's brain permanently scrambled, the decisions were up to me and I hadn't thought through potential threats. Pops woulda been pissed. I should have bought a portable grabber off the black market long ago.

With one hand, Mateo picked up an old V-8, nearly two-hundred seventy kilos of rusted heavy. He carried it to the disabled Bot-A and placed it to one side. Bending over the engine, he braced his three legs and adjusted his gyro-balance to push. With the V-8 between him and the bot's nanos—and any Puffers that were still active—he began shoving.

"You're loaded," Jagger said.

"Wand your hands," I instructed him.

"Why?"

"Just do it," I answered. Because I couldn't exactly say that he had touched my stuff and now was likely to die.

"Holy shit. You got a warbot," Jagger said, peering over my shoulder.

That I ignored.

Bot-B trundled into Aisle Alpha One behind Mateo.

"Behind you!" I shouted.

Mateo shifted. Lifted a lower limb. Fired. SS armor-piercing warheads took out the bot. Mateo's cybot limb flexed with the recoil, nearly knocking him over the engine. He corrected his balance and kept pushing Bot-A, not touching it himself. Hoping the extra distance would keep him free of nano contamination. He wasn't even breathing hard when he said, "In position. Leaving the Bot and the V-8 for AntiGrav decontamination. Going after Bot-B."

I positioned the AG Grabber over the Crawler and the engine and waited. Our two minutes were nearly up. The Bots' nanos would activate in seconds.

Using an electric engine this time, Mateo shoved the second Crawler over, stacked the electric engine on top, and went back with a steel-bristle broom and a heavy-duty dustpan sufficient for picking up hemp-plaz and synth-metal parts.

"Ten seconds," I warned. He emptied the scoop under the Grabber and stepped away. "Frying it," I said.

The Grabber lifted the thousand kilograms, give or take, as easily as it had lifted the Puffers. I set it to cook for an hour—which would leave us with a lot of time we couldn't fry other stuff, but I couldn't see another option. The energy usage was draining my reserves. Timing was going to be dicey, but the sun was still up and the solar panels all showed green. They hadn't been hit by the weapons fire, so I was still collecting energy. "What about you?" I asked—meaning what do we do about any nanos that might have infested Mateo's warbot body. Again.

"Running diagnostics," he said. "I'll set the suit to scan me every hour. If I see something, I'll cut it off and you can fry it. Then I'll reassemble it."

Mateo sounded calm and matter-of-fact. Clearly, he had been thinking about protocol should he ever be infested again. He hadn't freaked when I mentioned Puffers. He was doing good. Real good. That said a lot about his improving mental capabilities and health. I'd spent a lot of money on Berger-chip plug-ins to help restore his brain and give him back his memories. Money well spent.

"Copy that," I said. "Keep me informed."

"Got another batch of cats on a Puffer," he said. "Screen forty-seven."

I flipped to that screen and saw four cats, all female, stalking a Puffer. The Puffer was a little larger than most, with a square device on top instead of a weapon. That made it a recon-Puffer. It was hiding under a shipping container full of folded flight wings—part of a batch I had lucked into last month and hadn't gotten around to unpacking. The shipping container made a nice shady resting place for the Puffer. It also allowed the cats to slink up on it unobserved by any sensors on the Puffer's carapace.

Jagger leaned in closer beside the defensive control seat. The scent of sweat and sunscreen and engine oil and road dust and cigar and *man* wafted from him—a remembered scent, distant but . . . *interesting*. I breathed him in. My own, no-longer-strictly-human body reacted.

"What are they doing?" he asked.

"Hunting."

"But they're cats. They have to know there's no protein benefit to the Puffers. No caloric benefit either."

Because that was why cats hunted. Food. Normal cats, that is. I spared him a slant-eyed grin before returning to the screen. "Yeah, on the surface it's a waste of time. But a Crawler—an interloper—entered their territory, divided in two, had babies, and went after the source of their food and water. Me. In cat hierarchy, I successfully killed the Perker parents, proving I'm the alpha cat. Based on that evidence, they have to kill its babies or the babies may grow up and kill me. And they'll go hungry."

"You're implying the cats have intellect, the ability to reason, and sentience."

"Shining," Mateo warned in my ear.

My smile faded. Jagger already knew too much. He'd seen the office. Worse, he'd *touched* things in the office. No matter what happened, it was already too late for him. If he somehow lived, Mateo would want to take him out rather than let him tell the Outlaws what he'd learned. At best, if Jagger left the junkyard at all, it would have to be a vastly altered Jagger. I held in my sigh.

"Yeah," I said to Mateo and to Jagger, each for

their separate comments. "Watch."

The female cats were a mixed bag in terms of coloration—one with wide black and gray stripes; one with narrow, tone-on-tone gray stripes; one with orange stripes and a white spot under her chin; and one with splotches of brown and white and black. The tortoiseshell was the original matriarch of the pride; she had strange, long, bobcat-like tufts on her ears and one gimpy paw that had been partially amputated after a junkyard accident. I called her Tuffs because of the ear feathers and because she was . . . well . . . tough.

Most of the other cats were just called Cat. I wasn't imaginative with names and there were a *lot* of cats.

On the screen, Tuffs crouched on the edge of a stack of rear hatch doors. She looked at Wide Stripe, who belly-crawled a meter to her left. She looked at Narrow Stripe, who scooted back into deeper cover. The striped female cats were Tuffs' lieutenants, each one the primary breeder in one of the two prides. Tuffs looked at Spot, the female with the best vantage for ambush and a proven warrior; the orange-striped cat flicked her ear tabs, then leaped at the Puffer. A silent killing machine.

Spot landed on top of the Puffer, claws digging in as it bucked on its collapsible wheels. She rode it, flipping it over and leaping out of the way. The gray-striped cats launched from either side and latched onto the upside-down wheels, holding them. The Puffer was now immobilized, unable to right itself. Spot released her hold and slid to her feet, to begin a scent-reconnoiter. In less than a minute, she found the tiny seam where the Puffer had been sealed for active duty. She began to scratch around the seam, sensing with her claws. She went still and looked up at Tuffs. The matriarch tensed, her eyes fiercely intent.

Spot repositioned her body and dug in, releasing the seal. The Puffer bounced and twisted, pulsing its wheels. The striped cats pulled the Puffer apart. It stopped moving. When the cats were sure it was dead, they pulled it into the middle of Aisle Tango Three and sauntered off.

Tuffs looked directly at the camera and licked her lips, making a demanding *mrower* before she turned her back on me and jumped high, to a skid full of ship anchors. Tracking her hunters from above, she followed as they searched for more prey.

"That's . . ." Jagger went silent.

"Shining," Mateo said, with his metallic sigh.

"Yeah. I know," I said to them both.

"You have sentient killer cats. *And* you have a warbot," Jagger said, in awe, going back to the most important part.

"Yeah." I'd have to change Mateo's name if I introduced them. Something similar, maybe, like Matt.

On the next screen, a Puffer appeared. It was a grenade launcher mini-bot. Jagger reacted quickly and shot it to pieces. I notified Mateo, who went to pick it up. Another Puffer appeared and was shot down by Jagger. Another. And another. My new pal seemed to be having fun.

Jagger moved closer to me, again watching the screens over my shoulder. It felt odd to have him there. Comforting and frightening and something else I had pushed away from my life and decided I'd never experience again. His scent was sweat-ripe and cigar-strong, tainted by the tang of engines and gasoline, that rare OMW scent that made me *want*. . . .

I stopped myself right there. Unless Jagger survived the transition and I managed to alter his memories, he was a dead man walking.

"Warbot," I said to Mateo. "Can you gather up the parts and add them to the frying Crawlers? Without getting your suit infected?"

"Roger that. Can do."

But he didn't sound happy about it. Or rather, he didn't sound happy about our visitor, who could have slit my throat at any moment for the last—I checked my chrono—half hour while I defended the junkyard. And he hadn't. Jagger was—for certain—one of the good guys. And that broke my heart.

"What's his name?" Jagger asked.

I swiveled my chair to him, thinking Jagger was asking about Mateo, but found my visitor peering into the med-bay. I removed the war-sleeve—which hurt like a *mother* as it disconnected—and joined him. I pulled on gloves as I moved. It was likely too late, but . . . maybe?

"He's Notch. Because of the notched ear."

"The cats have sentience. And some sort of group communication. Like ESP," he said. "Like those birds that move in concert in flight and look like living clouds. Or fish in the ocean."

"Seems so. No way to prove it."

"You could catch them. Have them taken for study."

Which someone might want to do to me, now that I'd broken cover.

"No."

Jagger's eyes met mine and he smiled. Up close, his eyes were a dozen colors—pale-milk-chocolate brown and green and, in one, a tiny spot of blue. In the confines of the office, he was taller than I had thought, broader. His scruff of beard was maybe two days old. And *bloody hell,* that achingly familiar scent. His hand lifted and I thought he might remove my orange glasses. Something inside my chest did somersaults as my entire system responded to a man I didn't even know. Carefully, deliberately, I stepped back and didn't touch him.

"I respect that," he said, dropping his hand. "Warrior honor."

Unsettled, I bumped into the fridge, used it as an excuse, opened two more beers, wiped them both with a skin wand, and set one for him on the table at the dining booth.

I had stripped the booth from a high-end RV and it, along with the RV bed, were intended to hide what the office really was. From Jagger's reaction, I wasn't sure I had succeeded. Taking the beer, Jagger stood beside the leather bench at one side of the booth, opened the bottle, and took a swig. Then took a step toward me. And another.

"Well, you gave me a couple beers and entertainment." His eyes sparkled, like milk-chocolate fireworks. "Best battle I've been part of in weeks. As first dates go it's been pretty good."

He stopped in front of me. Close. Too close. The progression of the bottle to my mouth didn't stutter but it was a near thing. Bottle rim at my lips, I said, "Date? Kinda presumptuous there, Asshole."

Jagger laughed, the sound filling the office, vibrating in my chest and lower, into the part of me that felt . . . something. Something full of need and loneliness.

"When your kutte's tracking sensor went off, we took bets if it was really you. Shared photos from back then. Told stories. I can see the twelve-year-old Shining in your grown-up features. Pointed chin, high cheekbones. Eyes."

This time he did reach for my glasses. I seized his wrist with a gloved hand, stopping him. His hand was tanned and dark and had long black hairs that curled at the knuckles. He stopped, his hand only centimeters from my face.

"Seeing as Shining Smith just won me a month's wages, I figured least I could do is buy you dinner and a movie," he finished.

"Not my name," I said, ignoring the kutte situation, and pushing at his mind with my blood. If he was already being infected with my own special nanobots, I'd be able to alter his thoughts.

Into my earbud, Mateo said, "Setting the screens for auto-load so you can follow the cats. Consider it entertainment on your *date*." And, yeah. There was some major snark this time.

"I don't date Outlaws," I said, pushing harder. "I remember Mama's boyfriend too much."

I didn't date, period. Not in years, not that I'd say that. It would come across as even more of a challenge. Outlaws *did* love a challenge, and being told "no" was a major dare. I didn't know him at all, but somehow, I knew Jagger wouldn't use force. Instead I would become his goal, to wheedle, charm, pursue, stalk, and court—what an OMW made-man would do to get whatever or whomever they had been denied.

Jagger pulled from my grip, walked back, and sprawled on the bench seat, one knee bent, his boot heel on the wood beneath the leather cushion. Another man might have put his boot on the leather itself. Something about the consideration made me like him and I couldn't afford to like him.

"Ladies tell me I'm *adorable*," he said.

"Old Ladies are biker chicks. Not me." I wasn't and never would be an Old Lady. That was a term for one of the women who married into the Outlaws or became a longtime girlfriend. I was not a goal to win or a woman to pursue. I was way more than that.

His expression shifted and he sat upright, sliding his hand along my table, where my own hands had been at breakfast. *Oh, bugger.* It had been less than twelve hours since I sat there, ate there, my hands on the surface. And I hadn't wiped it down.

"Oh," he said. "Yeah. I never thought about how that might sound to you. You did what the rest of us couldn't. You stopped the Mama-Bot. You saved our butts and earned the patches to prove it. Sorry."

"Don't have the slightest idea what you're talking about." But I did. I was Little Girl. I was the only living female made-man in the Company at the time. I'd paid my dues. Lost everything. Nearly died. And saved the warriors of three chapters and a battalion of Uncle Sam's fighters from certain destruction. I'd been awarded my kutte, elevated in status, and honored. And then Pops died and the nanobots I had been in-fected with proved to be too dangerous. So, I van-ished.

My nanobots—the mutation I carried and the in-fection I transmitted—were why it was already too late for Jagger.

Feeling the gloves on my hands, knowing they looked strange in this setting, I tossed Jagger a pack-age of processed cheese crackers and sat opposite him.

"No fresh food," I said, hiding the fact that I had a greenhouse, just as I hid so much else. "And no get-ting out of here. Not until the Puffers are all gathered and destroyed."

"What about my bike?"

I shrugged. "Soon as the sun recharges my bat-teries, I can decontaminate it before you leave."

"Leave? We leave together."

"If that was an invitation, it lacked a certain charm, Asshole."

"Shining—"

"That sounds like a name. It's not mine. Eat your crackers."

Into my earbud, Mateo said, "Make a decision and make it soon."

I didn't tell him the decision had probably already been made.

I drank my beer. Ate the cracker Jagger passed

me, sharing from his pack. We settled back and watched the screens as the cats skulked around the junkyard in small groups, killing Puffers. Mateo followed the mayhem and destruction, gathering up the bot remnants and taking them to the AG Grabber to fry. AG Grabbers were pre-war tech. A lot of other stuff on the property was war tech and I was not supposed to have it. Like Mateo's warbot suit, the only thing keeping my friend alive.

"Who's the warbot?"

"Don't know his real name," I lied, speaking softly, slowly, pushing with my blood, continuing the attempt to alter his memories. "But I call him Matt. The boss, the owner of the junkyard, found him working as a slave in a town not far from here and brought him back here to live or die. He lived. Boss might know personal stuff, but Matt and I don't share histories or private info. At all."

"I like the modifications he made on his bot."

"He's good at what he does." Which carried a lot of unspoken threats. Threats Jagger understood, if the fleeting, challenging smile was an indication. *Really?* He'd challenge a warbot? OMW-dude was an idiot, on top of being an Asshole. A good-looking, almost-charming Asshole. I clenched my fists at the need to reach out and touch him.

He gestured to the screens with his beer. "Don't reckon you'd let me take pics of the scanners and screens."

"Nope."

"Don't reckon you'd let me make a vid of the cats hunting."

"Nope."

"And I assume you have the means and capabilities to make sure I don't take vid, or leave before you're ready, without your permission."

"Not bad, Asshole." I grinned at him. "Matt.

How's our visitor's bike?" I asked without raising my voice.

"Pretty li'l thing. Hope I don't have to hurt it," he said, over the office speakers.

Jagger's eyes flashed at the mention of hurting his bike, but he smiled anyway.

"I'll have to be on my best behavior."

"Good idea," Mateo said.

We sat in silence, watching the cats hunt and Mateo clean up. Time passed. Twice, Jagger spotted something and moved to the weapons. Shot a Puffer. Each time, Mateo collected and fried it. They were working together, silent. Which was a very bad sign for my own long-range problem solving.

The sun moved toward the west; the hottest part of the day passed into late afternoon. I made coffee. Opened a pack of dried apples to share. Jagger watched, his eyes on my gloved hands.

The med-bay light flashed three times and went dark. I got up to find Notch sleeping, breathing, his open wounds no longer open and most of his blood washed away. Med-bays weren't perfect but they were very, very good when the nearest veterinarian was thirty klicks away. I popped open the bay and used the disinfectant sprayer to wash off Notch—thin, red-tinted fluid gurgling down the drain. I dried off the unconscious cat and tapped the panel, saying, "Instructions for rehab."

The med-bay's androgynous computer voice said, "Clear liquids tonight and tomorrow. Minced protein after forty-eight hours. Commence swimming therapy at seventy-two hours. Reevaluation in seven days."

"Yeah. If I live that long," I muttered, laying non-fibrous padding over the thin, glued line of wounds, and wrapping the cat's torso in sticky wrap.

"Why wouldn't you live that long?" Jagger asked, his voice coming from behind me. Too close.

My breath caught. That earlier longing moved through me like a slow wave, unfurling, covering, drenching all of me.

"You ever make a cat swim?" I asked. "Not that I have water for cat-paddling. No one does, around here."

"Huh."

The med-bay was an older model, from before the change of weather patterns and the loss of fresh water. Its instructions didn't take the low-freshwater world into account.

"I'll keep him in the back airlock for forty-eight hours, feed him according to instructions, drug him when he gets too wild. When I can get the bandages off without getting myself mauled, I'll let him go. He'll live or not."

I glanced back and up to see Jagger watching my hands as I secured the tail of the wrapping. The sticky tape was bright purple. Notch would hate it. How I knew that, I didn't know. Most cats couldn't see the colors red and purple, except as shades of gray. All the junkyard cats were different.

"You've worked on cats before," Jagger said.

"Tuffs, Notch's primary mate, is a junkyard Torti," I said. "Her paw got stuck under a skid, early on in my employment here. Broke her leg. Crushed part of her paw. She was trapped and was fighting it like a rabid cat when I got there. She calmed down when I talked to her, explaining what I was going to do, not that I thought she understood me. But even with the explanation, she wouldn't let me touch her. I figured I'd have to shoot her, put her out of her misery. I went back to the office and got one of my employer's weapons—"

"One of dozens," Jagger said softly.

"It's a scrap and junkyard, Asshole, of course he has guns. Everyone all over the state has guns to protect us from roving bands of raiders. Boss makes a point to keep them out of the wrong hands. And anyway, by the time I stepped back through the airlock, there she was, sitting with her bloody paw to her chest, waiting on me. Along with four of the meanest cats you ever saw, from her first litter here. She had chewed off part of her own foot and come to me for help."

I stroked Notch's head. He'd nearly died today. All the cats had worked together to save the junkyard and help me. It was time for a sacrifice to the cats, so to speak.

Leaving the med-bay open, in the kitchenette I unsealed a pouch of goat's milk and poured it into a wide, shallow bowl. In another bowl, I dumped a pouch of very expensive chicken chunks and stirred in a helping of crunchy kibble. I un-gloved, scanned through the front airlocks, and when I was sure no Puffers were in the vicinity, I opened the locks and placed the bowls outside. Fast. The airlocks closed.

Lifting Notch, I carried him to the small space between the two back airlock doors. I got him settled in with an old army blanket and two bowls, one with water and one with canned broth. A shallow tray with desert dirt, suitable for a litter box, went on the other side of the floor. I added a folding household ladder that should be easy to climb and would let him see out as soon as he felt like making the few steps up. I sealed the lock, leaving the sleeping cat safely between the two back airlock doors.

"You were telling me about Tuffs," Jagger said.

He was back at the med-bay, a fresh beer in his hand. He hadn't asked, but since he was effectively a prisoner, I didn't begrudge him the stout.

"I told her she could come in, but her kits had to wait outside. I explained that I'd put her in a box and she would go to sleep and she'd wake up better. Not healed. But better."

"You talked to the cats." Deadpan. Not laughing.

I shrugged and ran a hand wand over my hands, cleaning them.

"She came in, let me lift her into the med-bay, and lay down. When the surgery was over and she woke up, she limped to the kitchen, demanded goat milk, drank it and went to—the owner's bed." I had almost said "my bed."

Jagger seemed to find my inept lies amusing and breathed out a laugh.

"The boss slept on the dinette bed for three days until Her Majesty decided she was well enough to leave."

"And where did you sleep?"

My lips lifted in a small smile. I turned from the sink to see Jagger cleaning the med-bay. I was so surprised I stopped dead. He knew his way around, cleaning with disinfectant and refilling the surgical supplies from the marked cabinet to the side. He hit the right sequence for decontamination on the instruction screen and ultraviolet light lit the room. It was scut work, not the sort of thing a National Enforcer did.

"I live in Naoma," I said, naming a nearby town.

Jagger made a noncommittal sound. As he worked, the sun set, and the office darkened. The modified, low-water-use air-scrubber plants closed their leaves and stopped removing pollutants from the air. The lights overhead should have blinked on, bright and gleaming. Instead, they came on slowly, with a dull glow, a brownout that indicated the office AI, nicknamed Gomez, had shunted power to the med-bay and the AG Grabber. I'd overused my energy supply and now I was paying for it. Between the Grabber's power usage and healing Notch, my energy reserves were nearly tapped out. I could draw on the spaceship's nearly inexhaustible supply, but . . . No.

Not with Jagger here. I had already used the shields, but they were less obvious to humans; I was sure he hadn't noticed, beyond a weird crawly feeling under his skin. But if I used the Weakly Interacting Massive Particle power from the *SunStar*'s engines or the office's weapons array, he'd figure it all out. I didn't think even my talents could make Jagger forget a WIMP engine, and if I couldn't alter his memories, Mateo would kill him to protect us. And . . . I didn't want Jagger dead. *Bloody damn.* I didn't want him dead.

On the screens, I saw pride cats targeting a line of Puffers on Aisle Tango Three. I counted fourteen cats and six Puffers, most of them weaponized. Even with those numbers, that was not good odds for the cats.

"I have jerky and dried fruit at the bike," Jagger said, tucking his fingers into his pockets, looking all relaxed and loose and easy, as if he couldn't kill me with those hands in less than two seconds if he wanted. "But since the bike is outside and I'm not, may I impose on the hospitality of Little Girl to let me use her facilities and to feed me?"

That was about as formal as an OMW ever got. When he didn't change his stance or his expression, I jutted my chin at my PTC, my personal toilette compartment.

"I'm not that little, but help yourself. As to food" —I tilted my head, thinking about my supplies—"Boss has pouches of tuna, canned shrimp, and goat's milk. A couple of tablespoons of butter, a few dried herbs, onion powder, a little wheat flour, and roasted garlic." As an afterthought I added, "Canned corn. Salt. Pepper."

Jagger grinned ear to ear. The transformation was startling and intriguing and *ho-ly cow.*

"Little Girl, that sounds like the makings of a sea-food stew, right here in the middle of the West Virginia desert."

I had no idea why I offered my hard-to-replace and terribly expensive foodstuffs to the National Enforcer. A small voice—not the Berger-chip implant, but a recognizable, small voice—whispered into the back of my mind, *Because you're lonely*. That stopped me cold.

The voice was right. Mateo and I had been alone for years. I was no longer human. And Mateo was a warbot, as much a machine as a man. Except for limited and brief times, he wasn't someone I could see or touch or physically interact with.

Jagger was human. Jagger was *here*. Right now.

Chances were very good that he'd be dead or different—altered—in seventy-two hours tops. First time in forever, I had company. If I'd admit to being Shining Smith, he'd be company who knew the real me and what I had done, or at least some of my history. He'd be company who could talk to me about the Outlaw Militia Warriors and the outside world. Real conversation. Maybe a game of cards. An old movie.

But if he'd sent Harlan, if he was the traitor, he might also just shoot me and be done with it.

The loneliness ached. *Take it,* the small voice said.

I opened my mouth, still trying to decide.

"I don't know who your Shining Smith is. My *boss*'s name is Smith but the only thing shiny on him is his bald head."

"Your *boss*? Really."

I ignored him and turned away, leaving him hulking behind me. He didn't strangle me or cut my throat, heading for the PTC instead. Score one for Jagger.

Though it was hard to see in the dim light with the orangey glasses, I opened the food supply cabinet and removed the ingredients, putting it all on the counter. Jagger returned from the PTC too fast to have used the body wand, not that he had clean clothes to change into. I thought about that while he raided my cabinets to find a two-gallon stew pot, which he placed on the hob, and turned on the propane stove. He began to assemble the stew, starting with the dried onion, butter, and canned seafood. All that in the office—in my house. Making himself at home. Doing things I'd done alone for years.

I didn't know what to do with myself.

I decided to clean up. After the fight, I stank. I left the room.

I stood in the tiny toilette, adjusting the screen to show the views from the office cameras, watching Jagger in case he decided to snoop. He didn't. But he moved well—economical and sure. As I watched, I used the body wand. Dead skin cells, dried sweat, body hair, and desert filth landed in the bottom of the stall. I blew my body clean with the small blower and palmed a little dry shampoo into my hair, rubbing it into my scalp before vacuuming it.

I missed water. I missed it a lot.

And I needed to make a decision about Jagger. Fast.

After the wanding, I cleaned up my mess, moisturized, put on my orangey lip gloss and Kajal, and dressed in clean clothes, things I could sleep in comfortably if it came to sharing quarters with him. With Jagger. Who was clearly a dangerous mountain of a man. I stared at myself in the mirror, my glasses off, my odd orange eyes staring back at me. In the low light of the brownout, it wasn't likely that Jagger could see my eyes anyway, so I didn't *have* to wear the lenses. Hopefully. I debated putting on Little Mama's perfume. Makeup.

This was not a date. It wasn't.

But some small part of me might want it to be.

And the deadly part of me demanded it to be. I squashed that part down.

Back in the main room I defaulted all the inside screens, including the one in the PTC, to show outside events. I pulled out some of Pop's clothes, things he'd worn before the war, before the stress and constant battle and seeing people he loved die had stripped all the meat off him, leaving him a shell of his former self. Before the Parkinson's stole his brain and personality and memories. And before I changed. I rested my hand on the heavy fabric. The pants legs would be too short, but they were soft and clean. Better than the sweat-stained things Jagger was wearing now.

Jagger had made a roux with the butter and flour and herbs, added in the goat milk, dry milk, a bottle of water, and the seafood from their packets. It wasn't fresh seafood from the ocean, which I hadn't had since I escaped Washington State and headed east, but it smelled delicious.

I placed the clean clothes in the PTC. Jagger set the propane burner to simmer and went to the toilette. Shut the door. I hadn't said a word. Into my earbud Mateo said, "Got yourself a servant. That's a little fast even for you."

Softly I replied, "I didn't do that on purpose."

"Did he touch you?"

"No." I thought through the events of the afternoon. "But the office hasn't ever been decontaminated. And I didn't wash my hands at lunch. Or after I set up the med-bay. I never thought about it. I don't clean my stove or the cabinets."

"You're still passing them through your sweat," Mateo said. "Interesting."

And awful. We had hoped I'd eventually stop secreting the funky nanobots through my pores.

My ant-stung wrist itched, wanting to be used, as if the nanos knew what was happening and wanted to speed things up.

Night fell. On low-light cameras I watched the

pride cats tear into another Puffer. I couldn't ID the specific cats, but they were fierce. I watched as Mateo strode in, lifting his long legs over the skids of engine and body parts, and swept up the pieces.

"Gomez," I said, talking to the office AI. "Put on some of Pops' music in the background." Pops had loved music of all kinds: Heavy Metal bands, nineteen-forties Big Band, Jazz, R-and-B, crooners, Country, even the skirling early-war martial Celtic stuff. He listened to everything. Eclectic taste. Gomez started with a tear-jerker called "Half as Much" by Rosemary Clooney.

"Makes it easier," Mateo said, picking up where he left off. "We won't have to burn the body. I'll come up with the cover. Meantime don't admit to being Shining. If he lives, it would make it harder to mind-wipe him. From now on, your name is Heather Anne Jilson."

"I don't look like a Heather Anne," I grouched.

"Tough." The printer began spitting out documents. "Heather Anne Jilson was the name of the girl whose mother was being beaten up by Darson, the one saved by an enforcer. The one who supposedly died in the Battle of Seattle."

His brain didn't work on every level all the time, but Mateo was thorough about security. Sometimes scary thorough. I paged through the thin brown hemp-docs on the printer. Heather now had a full ID, background, and history, all documented. I stuffed the docs into my personal storage area and pulled out my kutte. I hadn't looked at it in ages and it was way too small to fit now. I'd been spider-monkey small at twelve and had put on a quarter meter and a few kilos since then. I pulled off the old sensors, found the one that was activated when the Crawler crossed over the property boundary, and ripped it off. I put them all into a box. I added some older sensors and a few ancient digital camera parts. Some early EntNu Coms, earth-to-space hardware. The box now looked as if I stored small electronic scrap in it.

I placed the box on the cabinet, knowing that the decision on how to proceed had been made for me the moment Jagger started to serve me. It was a damn shame. He was interesting. But he'd live or he'd die. Either way, I couldn't keep him around and I had to make sure he remembered what I wanted him to.

I set the table for two. Which was really weird. I had never done that before. I checked the power levels on the office weapons that Jagger didn't know about yet. Stirred the soup. Realized I was nervous. There were little pinpricks all over me and my wrist was all but buzzing. My system was flooding with battle pheromones and mating chemicals and my breath rate and heart rate were increasing. I fought to push my reaction down, to control my anxiety and my need, to decrease the secretions of chemicals and nanos through my pores.

I was never around people for long. I made sure that I never had to deal with this part of me. I didn't have the control I might have if I went into town more often.

"So. I'm Matt?" Mateo said, making sure I had chosen.

"Yeah. Matt," I said flatly. "I didn't mean to transition Jagger."

"You never do."

"A transition is better for him than being dead. If I can alter his memories enough to keep us safe," I amended.

"If he lives through the process, maybe," Mateo said, his metallic voice managing to convey both doubt and mockery.

I rubbed my wrist and said softly, "That was mean."

But Mateo was right. Surviving the transition was no sure thing. Yet I had lived through it twice.

The first time was when I was twelve, near the end of the first year of the war. I was swarmed by deadly genetically-engineered male ants. They bit off parts of me and stung me full of poison. Then the queen got me, depositing her DNA-based bio-nano-bots. The bio-nanos entered my bloodstream and attacked me on the genetic level—just as they had been designed to do to the ants. When I somehow survived the initial transition, the bio-nanos continued to modify me.

In the second incident, I got exposed to a different kind of nano when a bigger, newer model Chinese Mama-Bot crawled out of the bay and attacked what was left of Seattle. I'd been the only OMW small enough to get inside the Mama-Bot in an attempt to disable it. Once inside, I'd been attacked by Puffers, and their mechanical nanos—mech-nanos—got into a cut. The bio-nanos already in my system adapted and modified them too.

I'd survived the two transitions but they had left me what I was now—not superhuman, but no longer *just* human. With abilities that humans didn't have.

Eventually the half-bio/half-mech-nanos began to secrete through my skin, driven to seek out and modify others. All but one of the people I'd accidently or purposely touched after that had died in their own transition process. Including my father, who I had tried to save from the disease that had been sucking the life out of him.

And now I'd gotten sloppy and let a human into my space. Jagger was already showing signs of the transition, bending to my will, becoming what I called a thrall. And he didn't even have the fever yet.

Sloppy. I'd gotten *bloody* sloppy.

I got out playing cards and checked the Chrono

because it felt as if my visitor had been in there a long time, but ten minutes wasn't long unless I was nervous. Then it felt like forever. The music switched to Frank Sinatra singing "Fly Me to The Moon." The music was changing again when I heard the PTC hatch open.

I didn't turn around. I stirred the soup, my toes tapping to Aretha Franklin belting out "Rolling In The Deep." When I did look over, Jagger was sitting at the dinette, dressed in Pops' clothes, his eyes on me, a fresh beer in one hand.

"Gomez. Music volume down. Matt," I said over the office speakers, pushing with my blood slightly, accepting Jagger's transition, preparing for enough mind-altering to allow him to leave us alive. "Update, please."

"Twenty-four Puffers accounted for. Jagger's bike is fine, to this point, Heather. What are you and Jagger having for supper?"

Small talk. Baby steps, using our fake names to overwrite Jagger's short-term memories with new ones. We chatted about the cats. We mentioned the imaginary boss a few times and his imaginary trip into Charleston, West Virginia, on business. Jagger didn't take part. I brought the stewpot to the table and ladled chowder into the bowls. Jagger didn't ask about the name changes. Didn't seem to notice. He'd touched everything I had touched in the toilette. The beers. The ladle . . . everything.

We'd had a guest once before, the first year I was here, Grant Zuckerman, a nice man who showed an interest in me and who I liked. A lot. He and I got close. Very close. It seemed like an okay thing, since Grant lived in the nearest town, Naoma, and had Internet access and wanted to do business with the scrapyard. Mateo and I had done great with the mind-altering, giving Grant his freedom, keeping him coming back, or so we thought. Unfortunately, Grant wanted more. It had gotten ugly. Mateo had been forced to end him. The bones were out back, buried beneath a pile of rusted-out John Deere tractors, his flesh long since eaten by rats.

Transitioning the cats had been a mistake. I hadn't known the bastardized nanos could pass from human to another species, but it had gone better once we figured out that Tuffs had become mine, and a queen. The cats didn't seem to get sick. They just got better, smarter, faster, and had the ability to communicate mind-to-mind.

I brought spoons to the table and sat. We ate, and the fish stew was delicious.

"So. While we wait on Matt to clean out the Puffers," I said, "tell me why you're here."

Jagger frowned.

"You said there was a tracking sensor?"

"On a kutte," Jagger said, sounding uncertain.

"That's a biker riding leather. A vest."

He nodded, the motion jerky. His color was higher than before we ate, his temperature beginning to rise.

"My boss got in a pile of miscellaneous stuff not long ago." I got up and brought the box of junk to the table. Placed it beside Jagger. "We can dicker—info, updates, and a little cash in return for your sensor—if it's in here."

Jagger frowned again, but he went on eating. Several bites later he said, "Good fish stew, considering we're in the wilds of nowhere desert. What info do you want?" He hadn't even looked into the box.

I said, "You can tell me what happened to Darson and his friend Buck Harlan." Darson, the man who had been beating his girlfriend and her daughter—who was now me. Buck Harlan, the man whose body I left burning in the Tesla. Building upon things we had talked about and things I still needed to know. Replacing memories. Binding him to me through a shared chemical, hybrid nanobot signature.

Building my nest, just like the cats did.

Just like the bicolors did.

As we ate, Jagger told me about the Battle of Seattle, and the deaths of Darson, his girlfriend, and her daughter. I corrected his memory and said I, Heather, had gotten away. I made up a few details, enough for his own mind to build upon, unless he looked at it all too closely. We had seconds of the fish stew, finishing all but a half cup. I wouldn't be making fish stew again in many months, unless I sold some valuable scrap, especially since this problem with Harlan meant I hadn't gotten my black-market goods. My eyes felt raw at the thought of Harlan. Dead, protecting me. What did Asshole know about Harlan's death?

My voice rough, I asked, "And Buck Harlan?"

"He went missing two weeks past."

Jagger lounged back and stretched out his long legs on the bench, crossing his bootless feet, wearing Pops' socks. It was strange to see a man in my father's clothes. Jeans, double layers of t-shirts bulging with weapons in a harness. Those socks. Striped bright green, dark blue, and silver—Seattle Seahawks colors. Pops and Little Mama and I used to go to the games. I hadn't seen a live football game in years. Pops used to keep a can of Skoal in his back pocket, apple blend or vanilla. I could almost smell the flavored tobacco. He used to sing to Aretha's music. He had a terrible voice. Grief welled in me so fast that tears pooled in my eyes. I turned aside and blinked them away.

All sorts of things were simmering to the surface and making me feel weird.

Without cleaning my hands, I gave Jagger another beer, more of my sweat on the damp bottle. The man could really hold his alcohol—all that body mass meant it took a lot to get him drunk. He removed the top and took a long pull before setting it on the table, his hands smoothing the bottle around and around, his fingers brushing where I had touched it. *Foolish, foolish man*, that little voice whispered.

"Harlan was tracking down info about an influx of MS Angels back into Louisville."

I went still. *Mara Salvatrucha Angels*. They had been the scourge of . . . well, of everything and everyone. MS13 had merged with the Hell's Angels in a hostile takeover in 2030, creating a biker arm of the international criminal gang. The newly merged gang had swept through large swaths of territory, leaving a path of property destruction and dead bodies in its wake, an onslaught so violent that only the Outlaws had been equipped to counter it. The biker clubs went to war in 2032, in what had ended up a nasty, decade-long internecine conflict, led by a very young Pops and his predecessor. Pops had won and the scattered remnants of the MS Angels had not ended up as his best buddies.

And now Harlan was here, dead, at the hands of a traitor, probably working with the PRC—the enemies of the Gov. and of me. Had the MS Angels found Pops' famous Little Girl? A sense of foreboding grew, one I tried to keep off my face as I asked, "OMW cleaned the Angels out in 2040, didn't they?"

"Little known fact. The remnants of the MS Angels allied with the PRC late in the war. And after the war, when the Chinese departed, the Angels started to rebuild. They had Chinese tech and weapons caches. The post-war famine opened up territory. We heard rumors they were expanding again, this time without, or in front of, the People's Republic of China, but with their own brand of ferocity and violence. Harlan went to check them out."

Bugger. I didn't know what to do now. If the MS

Angels had taken down Harlan and sent his body to me, that meant they knew who I was and at least some of what I had on site—the post-war military weapons caches for starters. And if the Angels had PRC tech, then . . . might they also have sent the Crawler?

Bugger damn . . .

Panic pattered up and down my spine. On the screen, I watched as the junkyard cats tore into another Puffer. My thoughts still turned inward, I asked slowly, "Do you have a pic of Harlan? A recent one?"

"Why?" Jagger asked, as he peeled a Morphon off his wrist. The chameleon capabilities of the narrow wrist band had matched his skin so perfectly I hadn't even noticed it until he twisted it off, snapped it flat, and unfolded it. I hadn't seen a Morphon in ages; I still used an old model Hand-Held. No one had Morphons except the military, the Gov., and a few filthy rich citizens with the proper sat-dishes. The Morphon, like the bike Jagger rode and all the tech on it, was an indication of the deep relationship between the military and the OMW.

Holy freaking bugger. The MS Angels, the OMW, the military, and the Gov. all probably knew where I was. I was so screwed.

Jagger swiped through pics and handed me the Morphon. It felt silky in my palm and instantly matched my much darker tanned skin. On the face of the Morphon was a pic of Harlan and Jagger, their bikes in the background.

I pushed the Morphon back and pulled my Hand-Held. I found the stills of the Tesla and the body of the OMW in the back, then handed it to Jagger.

"This came today, packaged and shipped inside a piece of scrap the owner bought. It's Harlan, isn't it?" Harlan, who had been my go-between for the OMW, the black-market network, and the real world. Harlan, who had been hunting for traitors.

Jagger flipped though the stills several times, his face giving nothing away.

But he had already entered the transition. I could feel the way his heartrate sped and his adrenaline spiked.

"I recognized the tats as OMW," I said. "When you showed up, I thought you might have sent him. Some kind of message to my boss. Then the Crawler situation happened and you were in as much danger as I was, so, I'm now assuming the reason you came had to be for something else, maybe even the kutte sensor you talked about."

Jagger transferred accusing, angry eyes to me. Any confusion or acceptance or transition uncertainty was gone in the adrenaline rush. He was back to himself for a moment.

"You let me into your inner sanctum? Your *shelter*?" It was an accusation and also the dawn of the protective instincts created by the transition. "A stranger who showed up on your doorstep the same day a dead man came calling?"

A dart hit the back wall a half centimeter from his head. Jagger went for his weapon.

"Don't," Mateo said through the speakers. Jagger went still, eyes burning with rage.

I took back the Hand-Held and tilted my head to the dart.

"I was never in danger."

"So, you lured me in here. You were never in danger from me," Jagger stated, "but I'm in danger from Matt and the internal defensive systems."

"I let you in to keep you safe from the crawlers. But if you sent Harlan to me, dead and covered with bicolors, then yeah."

"And if I didn't?"

"Then . . . I have a really bad feeling that the

Angels are heading this way. Probably tonight."

Jagger might wonder why the MS Angels wanted to kill Heather-whatever-her-name-was. My lies were in danger of falling apart. Scrambling, I said something that made sense. "They must want some of the tech here, or the weapons."

"You have weapons?"

"A few," I said. "Some of the boss's scrap is military scrap."

My mind zinged from one thought to another. If the Angels had gotten their hands on a Chinese Crawler, and on Harlan, maybe they planted the bicolors on Harlan's body. Figured they'd swarm me, kill me, so they could take the junkyard and its goodies. Two birds with one Tesla. The Angels were crazy enough.

"Matt," I said, "update."

"Remote Viewing Aircraft have been aloft for hours. Sending one to the access road and one to reconnoiter the property. Vids to your main screen. Also searching outlying cameras."

"Nothing," I said, as the ARVACs' cameras took up the entire left half of the big screen. The road in both directions was empty. "What about a remote attack? An ARVAC of their own."

Jagger said, "If your weapons are important enough to warrant all the things you say they've done, then they'd want to see the whites of your eyes."

"Up close and personal," I said. "Yeah. Okay. Still. Matt?"

"Status quo," he said. "Wait. At the extreme edge of sensor range, I'm picking up . . . something."

I nodded, my eyes on the screens. "You can relax, Jagger," I said, pushing a little through my nanobots that were entering his bloodstream and nervous system. When nothing happened, I pushed harder.

Jagger shook his head, blinking. He lifted the brown glass bottle as if trying to see inside. "I'm . . .

feeling weird. I shouldn' be feeling 'is way." He tried to stand and didn't make it. "Wha' you do to me?" He thought I'd poisoned him. Instead, his temperature was going up and the transition nanos were reaching a critical mass.

Mateo said. "I confirm activity at fifteen klicks. And the Puffers are suddenly all converging on the office."

Jagger cursed and nearly dropped the bottle.

"Whada fu—?"

His hands clenched hard. His eyes fluttered closed and he slumped over the table.

I leaped to my feet, kicked off my house shoes, and punched open the armor bay that Mateo had moved out of the *SunStar* and installed in the office. The narrow niche unlocked with a soft sucking *whoosh* and I stepped onto the mounting pedestal, my feet perfectly centered in the outline. Turning my back to the armor suit, I sucked in a deep breath as Gomez took over the armor AI and began counting down. I closed my mouth and eyes and held utterly motionless, hands down and out to my sides, fingers spread.

"Initiating female auto-donning," Gomez said.

The armor positioning arm went around my waist, pulling me against the torso segment. My head rocked forward and back. The armor sections began snapping over my body, interlocking, repositioning against muscles and joints, expanding and contracting to fit me perfectly. Across my middle, down my legs, down my arms.

I suppressed the desire to fight it as the helmet and the face piece locked over me. Claustrophobia, memories from my own piece of hell, stabbed into me like knives. I forced myself to hold. Hold. *Hold* utterly still. The breathing tube slid between my lips and against my cheek and blew stale air into my mouth. I blew out that first puff with a relieved breath. Inhaled slowly on the second. Again. Again. I opened my eyes, looking out into the office through the suit's visual screen and sensors, seeing what the office really was, what it could really do. Pops' last gift to me, when he was dying and had figured out that I needed to leave the OMW. The glove sectionals encased my fingers. The armored boots snapped shut.

"Prepare for peripheral nerve engagement, left hand," Gomez said.

I swore, as miniscule needles, finer than acupuncture needles, pierced into my palms.

"Prepare for peripheral nerve engagement, right hand."

It too engaged.

"Son of a *bitch*," I said, adding a few comments about the engagement process. Gomez didn't seem to care what I thought about his parentage or his sex life. Probably a good thing that the AI wasn't sentient.

"Do you wish catheter and bowel removal collection to be initiated at this time?"

"No. God no." I'd made the mistake of saying yes the first time I'd tried this. Never again. I'd hold it 'til I busted first.

I was breathing. I was alive. I was protected in the lightweight, space-worthy armor worn by US military in space-going vessels. My heartrate began to slow.

"Liquid oxygen breathing supply required?" Gomez asked.

"No. Current Earth atmosphere, desert conditions, West Virginia."

"Limited oxygen available according to current specified atmospheric parameters," Gomez stated. "As measured by outside sensors, CO_2 percentages are abnormally high in current atmosphere. Atmospheric dust filters active."

"Acceptable," I said.

"Armor donning complete." The waist arm clicked back.

I stepped down to the floor. To see Jagger staring at me. Wide awake. With a gun pointing at my middle.

"Well, aren't you just full of surprises," he said calmly.

"Put down the weapon," I said. "Do not pick it up again."

Jagger put the fancy gun down. Cursed. Wide-eyed, he stared at the weapon, right there, but not available to him. He did not pick it up again.

"Go to sleep," I commanded. Jagger slumped again.

"Mateo?"

"We're dead without power. I'm moving out front, taking control of manual defenses. You'll have to get into the ship and reroute power."

Mateo meant for me to go into the crashed and damaged spaceship that had leaked hazardous particles for years, and transfer power from it to our batteries before our next unexpected visitors arrived. It was dangerous, as I remembered from my one tour through the ship. My armor was flimsy compared to the warbot, which had built-in weapons and shielding, so, yeah. He was better equipped to defend us if it came to that. And with the office out of power to run the weapons we had retrofitted, my defenses were useless to me anyway.

"CAIT will walk you through the procedures," he said.

Right.

"CAIT" was the spaceship's AI: Central Artificial Intelligence Technology. I wouldn't be doing this alone.

I raced out the back and stumbled over the ladder. Notch, sitting on the top step, his face turned to the window, looked over his shoulder at me. I let the inner airlock close, sealing us in together. Standing frozen.

"*Mrow. Siss.*" It sounded like a statement. A two-part statement. I didn't know his meaning, but it felt like, *Invaders. Dangerous*.

"Yeah. And more on the way," I said to him. "Mateo. We got a screen in here? If so, show Notch the attackers approaching."

"You and those damn cats."

A tiny screen over the exit door brightened, flashed, darkened, and resolved into the vision of the road out front. "Invaders," I said to Notch, knowing he understood a very little English, mostly stuff about food. "If they get onto the property, there will be no goat milk. No water."

"*Sisssss*," he said, this one angry.

"If the Puffers continue to replicate, there will be no more protein or kibble. And they will eat your young."

His mouth opened to show his canines, which were bigger than a normal housecat's. "*Sisssss*." Very defiantly pissed. Notch eased down the steps to the floor and walked to the outer airlock. Looked back over his shoulder and again at the door.

"Timmy fell in the well," I muttered, quoting a 2040 film about a modified cyborg Collie dog that could actually speak English. I opened the outer airlock. Much slower than his previous speed, and looking a little clumsy in the bandages he hadn't tried to chew off, Notch stepped out into the night. Limping, he disappeared into shadows. I closed the airlock and said, "Mateo, engage security protocols."

"Engaging. Get to the ship. Looks like our visitors have heavy armament."

I switched my face shield to auto and raced through the dark aisles, past tons of older, rusted skids of scrap ready to be bulk-shipped. Prewar heavy equipment scrap from the top-down mining that had removed entire mountain ranges to provide granite cabinet tops for homeowners and coal for the power industry. Farm tractors from when this area had been fertile land instead of flat granite. Alloy car bodies that no one would ever buy, not in this day of lighter hemp-based materials. The scrap back here was all old stuff that had been here when I got here, and would be here forever, the perfect disguise for what we really were.

In my face shield, a cat form showed bright golden red with body-heat, dropped six meters in front of me, and sat. I skidded to a halt.

"Tuffs? What the—?" Ahead, on an adjoining aisle I needed to take, cats attacked a Puffer, ripping it to shreds. "Oh. Is anyone hurt?" Tuffs didn't reply, not that I could have understood her if she tried.

Mateo's warbot body moved down the aisle on his modified three legs and scooped the busted Puffer into a bucket. "No more for now," he said to the cat. "The Grabber will be busy. Just keep track of them, don't kill them."

Tuffs moved to the side. I raced on, now seeing cats leaping from aisle to aisle and pile to pile, following me. Or leading me. Right to the ghillie-tech cloth that covered the side access hatch of the United States Space Ship *SunStar*.

Beyond the tarp Mateo had rigged over the entrance, the ship's exterior was still functional. Stars shone on the undamaged part, reflecting sky and desert and visions of the junkyard in the automated, actively-repositioning armor and Chameleon skin. It was effectively invisible unless someone stumbled on top of it or knew it was here and was looking for it. The ship had gone down in the middle of the war, in a major Earth-orbit battle. It had broken up and the front half landed here. For some reason it had never been found, even after the war ended.

My Berger-chip must have sensed my uncertainty, because it chose that moment to chime in:

The timeline leading up to World War Three was chaos. The tension created by stable WIMP engine technology—which led to active solar system colonization—was made worse with the appearance of Bug aliens in 2036 when a scout ship with some functioning technology crashed into the North Sea. The ship was captured by the EU and much of the alien tech was reverse engineered and shared with the United States and other allies. This new tech was later stolen by other countries—notably the People's Republic of China, which refined and improved the Allies' designs. The subsequent claiming and colonization of Mars resulted in a war that began in 2043 and ended when the Bugs appeared in large numbers and forced the peace treaty of 2045. Bugs divided Earth into major parties and some sub—

"Shut up," I told the Berger-chip.

A lot of earth-based human tech had been lost in the war. The *SunStar* had space-going war tech, and some of it was lost as well—except for what ended up right here. The office had even more dangerous tech. All of it was banned. The power sources and weapons, if used, could be identified from satellites. So powering the main WIMP engines would be dangerous; it might draw attention to the junkyard. Instead, I would slowly power up a backup engine, and even more slowly transfer power from the *SunStar* to my equipment, batteries, and pre-war weaponry that—I hoped —no one could trace. But first, I had to make the power transfer happen.

"Where did the Crawler get in?" I asked Mateo.

A single screen opened in the center of my faceplate, showing me a dusty, brownish, squat warbot, slowly crossing the border, the time-date marker a week ago. The original Crawler had all sorts of devices protruding from its carapace. There would have been dozens more devices and weapons inside on foldouts, all of them capable of independent drive and lethal measures. It was seventy-five or so centimeters high, less than that side to side and back to front, roughly squarish but with rounded edges. It was still that size when it entered the spaceship. What emerged three days later were two babies, each more than half the original's size. They had taken on mass. From the spaceship.

"It entered the exterior rear engine compartment," Mateo replied. "So far as I can tell, the Crawler never made it to the bridge or to engineering. It spent all its time in the shielding bay, breaking up a spy drone."

"Copy."

I input the code Mateo had set when we first accessed the ship—Mateo, four, eight, one, six, alpha tango delta. I placed a palm over the viber, and my face against the scanner. The hatch opened with a measured *whoosh* and I stepped inside. Four cats slipped in behind me, Notch's tail tip almost getting caught when the hatch closed with a sense of finality. He was moving great for a cat who had been nearly dead. The security lights began to glow as I opened the next hatch and entered the ship proper. The sensors showed green: a breathable atmosphere. Manually, I slid my faceplate aside. All the low-water-use air-scrubber plants in the niche boxes on the walls had died years ago, as evidenced by the metallic, stale scent of the air.

In a jarring, unexpected Southern accent, *Sun-Star*'s AI said, "Welcome home, girl. 'Bout time you came to visit again."

The accent was odd, but not something I had time to worry about now. I raced into the dimly lit ship, searching the glowing schematics on the walls for the engineering department, or what was left of it after the ship crash landed. The floors—decks?—weren't flat or horizontal and some had holes down to other levels; the ceiling tiles had shattered upon impact and were all over the floors, and the walls were cracked. All of it had worsened over time, making traversing the ship physically demanding and precarious. Sprinting down the halls (or decks, or passageways, or whatever space goers called them) was a little like racing over the blasted bedrock in the desert. I banged my shin into a chunk of wall.

"Bloody damn," I said.

"Watch yo' mouth," the ship's AI said over her speakers. Which nearly brought me to a stop.

Into my earbud, Mateo said, "Moving into position at front gate. Intruders approaching from the west. No human or mechanical aggressors noted from other directions. Barriers are up and functional, leading to a single defensive point. All tire shredders and tracked wheel-disrupters are up and functional. Office weapons are auto-trained on front entrance. But all automatic armaments and defensive measures are slow to respond. We are seriously low on power, Shining."

I dropped into the engineer's seat, hating that I was safe back here and Mateo was out front, facing an unknown onslaught alone. An attack with tech and hardware that might be better than what we could use—assuming the Angels had PRC weapons—and still stay hidden from sat-surveillance. I could only hope the upgrades we had done on Mateo's suit and on the property were going to be enough. I strapped in, knowing that CAIT's command center wouldn't respond unless all the I's were dotted and T's were crossed.

Mateo said, "Grabber in position. *Power*, Shining. I need *power*."

From his tone, his suit had injected him with enough 'roids and swamped him with enough synth-pheromones to enrage a rhino.

"Powering up *SunStar*'s miniaturized backup WIMP-anti-WIMP particle processor engine," I said, watching the readouts. "Ionized neodymium is present in sufficient quantities to generate antigravity and power. Initiating warmup on WIMP and transfer systems."

"Copy. Make it fast. ARVACs indicate it's not the Law. Not the Gov. It's . . . It's a private army."

"No doubt?"

"None."

"Starting power transfer to office batteries and direct power to your suit," I said. Over Mateo's comms I heard the roar of approaching engines. It sounded like a battalion. "Come on, come on, come on," I whispered to the particle processor. In the cold void of space, WIMP engines provided gravity for personnel and antigravity for propulsion and weapons, and it happened *fast*. On Earth, powering on a WIMP engine that fast—even a miniaturized backup engine—created extreme temperatures and stressed the ship, and powering it on slow meant we were dead. I nudged the power system up faster than was safe, knowing that if a military satellite with the proper scanning systems was watching this part of the desert, they'd see the system come on and they would know what had happened to the remains of their space ship. Also, the heat emissions would melt most of the junkyard if I left it on too long.

The office battery supply showed seventeen percent. Eighteen percent. Nineteen percent, climbing too slowly.

"Bloody hell. Hurry up!" I cursed.

"I warned you about the language," the ship's AI said. "'Sides. I'm doing the best I can."

"Shining," Mateo said softly. Too softly. "They're turning in. I need that power *now*."

Batteries showed twenty percent. *Finally*.

Through my armored suit, I whispered to Mateo and to Gomez, the office AI, "Fire primary defenses."

Gomez's metallic voice said, "Firing."

Mateo confirmed. The earth rumbled under my feet. Up into my bones. My teeth shook.

The office battery dropped to thirteen percent. To ten. To seven.

Primary weapons fire stopped. I nudged the transfer power system up higher and saw the office battery percentage rise to fifteen percent. Too low. Too slow. *Damndamnbloodydamn.* I stuck a ship earbud into my other ear. I was now tied into Mateo, Gomez, and the ship's AI.

"CAIT. Shining Smith in engineering command seat."

I heard a strange popping sound over Mateo's comms and glanced at the direct power to his warbot suit. It looked off. Something was wrong. I commenced a suit system diagnostic while also searching for a way to tie directly into the office's security system screens.

"You're leaking air and fluid," I told Mateo. "Your suit's power drain has increased to twelve above maximum drain. What's happened?"

Mateo didn't answer. Tuffs leaped to my chair and sat on the armrest.

"*Orrrowmerow.*"

"My thoughts exactly," I muttered to her.

The ship AI said, "Honey, would you like me to evaluate Mateo's suit diagnostics?"

I frowned. *Honey?* "Yes. CAIT. Run suit diagnostics. Mateo. Respond."

Mateo didn't.

I spotted a new switch, or rather an old retrofitted switch, part of the ship's ongoing repairs and modifications, stuff Mateo did in his off time. It clicked when I flipped it, and the office screens blinked on, merging with the *SunStar*'s screens.

"System override," the *SunStar*'s AI said. "Input screens from off-ship are now merged onboard, which is interestin' in a strange kinda way. Warning. Off-ship systems do not correspond to my natural *de*fault parameters."

"Deal with it," I told the AI.

"Dealin' is what I do best, darlin'. Attempting to harmonize non-complementary soft and hardware."

I touched the screens, shoving them around, searching for one that showed Mateo. I found it. And stopped. Mateo was on the ground, eighty meters from the entrance. Surrounded by Puffers.

"*Orrrowmerow*." Tuffs batted the screen. "*Orrrowmerow. Orrrowmerow. Orrrowmerow! Mowwww.*"

A dozen cats rushed toward Mateo, attacking the Puffers. More cats joined the fight. I looked at Tuffs, meeting her eyes. Hers were the green of fresh leaves and rainforest moss, things I remembered from my youth. She stared at me, as if seeing more than I could understand.

"How did you do that?"

She chuffed at me, a disgusted puff of sound.

"Okay then."

The ship AI said, "The warbot suit has been compromised, sweet thang. Sealing off inner suit chambers. And by the way, you can call me Jolene."

"*Jolene*? What happened to CAIT?"

"She's boring. Jolene is feisty, dontcha think?"

"I don't really have an opinion."

I swiveled back to the screens and searched for vid that showed me the junkyard's entrance. And found it.

One manned Spaatz mini-tank and three Joint Light Tactical Vehicles from various branches of the military—all decommissioned and painted in black chitosan—were stopped out front. "Someone's been stealing from Uncle Sam," I muttered. Or the military had stabbed the OMW in the back and allied with the MS Angels. That would suck. For now, the equipment was trapped in the spiked tire and track traps that Mateo had raised.

From what I could tell, the human component of the assault team hadn't expected resistance. Several had left the protection of their Tac vehicles and had begun trying to free the tires and tracks when Mateo and the office opened fire. Their armor hadn't survived the combined firepower. I counted four humans on the ground, unmoving. The mini-tank was rocking back and forth on its track system. The tank was heavily armored, was handled by a human, and had a missile system mounted on top. With Mateo down and the office defenses on standby until the batteries recharged, I needed to damage or immobilize the missile system. I also needed to knock out any drones they brought. If the Spaatz tank got free, it had firepower the office couldn't withstand without the particle shields up, and the mini-tank was small enough to maneuver around the aisles and find stuff it shouldn't.

I needed more power faster. The office systems' shields and the USSS *SunStar*'s power siggie could be seen from space if military satellites were currently actively looking for it, but I didn't have a choice.

I checked the batteries. Still too low.

I cursed foully. Tuffs looked at me and flicked her ear tabs, amused. Jolene said nothing.

"I really don't want to do this."

I didn't have implants to interact directly with the ship, so this was not gonna be fun at all. Taking a deep breath, I pulled off my armored sleeve and shoved my hand into the engineering command sleeve, screaming, wordless, knowing what was coming. The sleeve contracted around my hand, fast, painfully tight. Needles punctured into me and engaged my nervous system. It hurt. It bloody well *hurt*. My scream went up in pitch. My breath shuddered as I forced myself to accept the pain and the input and the sensory overload.

I was damaging my arm. I was bleeding. I would deal with the injury later.

"That wasn't the brightest thing you ever done, darlin'."

I grunted. I increased the WIMP production and shunted more power to the office batteries. I could power up the office defense system and the AG Grabber or I could use some of the scant power to launch the office's other ARVACs now and take longer to get the systems up and running.

I needed intel. I launched the flying drones and set them to auto-scan. The office went into brown-out again. Now I had 102 seconds until I had sufficient power transferred to activate the weapons and the Grabber. I hoped the intel was worth it.

Melded with Jolene, I pressed my eyes against the command faceplate showing me the ship's external sensors, as the AI searched the skies. I spotted one enemy drone. Locked on. Sliding my bleeding hand to the left, I engaged the weapons array that was least likely to draw satellite attention. I fired.

Silently, the ship's EntNu-based offensive laser array took it down.

Gomez said, "Alert. Armed incursion from the western boundary. Six, on foot."

I pulled up the office cameras and spotted the six-man team, armed with automatic rifles, making their way into an older section of the yard. The scrap there backed up to a series of mine cracks, the main one wider than most and a hundred meters deep or more. The rock there was rotten, hundreds of unstable cracks forming when an old underground mine had caved in. I had scanned the area once and found traces of arsenic, benzene, and toxic coal dust. I hadn't bothered to explore further. I had no idea what the invading team might be after.

"Do not engage," I told Gomez. "Maintain observation via ARVACs and stationary camera system."

For now, I let the invaders go, curious what they were looking for. Or maybe that was Jolene's curiosity. It was already hard to tell as her sensors merged with my senses.

"You need to let me merge fully with the extra-ship defensive system you're using, darlin'. This three-way we're having is not working for me."

Again, the accent threw me, but I let her merge into the office AI.

"Oh. My. Ain't you jist the cutest li'l thang," Jolene said to the AI. "Gomez. Nice name. Your English translated coding ain't the best or the brightest but a lonely gal sometimes has to make do."

"Flirt later," I muttered. Far faster than I could have before, my mind slipped into the office vid scanners and checked around. There were more strangers in the junkyard, these close to the office. Two humans were at the rear office airlock. I fired everything I had at them. They went down. I slid through the screens, searching for more movement.

In the aisles, two cats were down and in pieces. I checked Mateo. He was still down. Eight Puffers were down near his suit, but as I watched, a Puffer pried apart an ankle seam in one of the three fully automated warbot legs. A second Puffer fired a small caliber weapon into the under-armor, round after round. "No," I whispered. I counted eighteen rounds, a full mag for the Puffer. The first Puffer rolled back and tore into the opening. They were working together. That was freaky.

"Now that ain't normal," Jolene said. "Puffers

talkin'? Dang. Next thang you know they'll be having tea and crumpets."

I had no idea what a crumpet was. It sounded like a good name for an insect, one I'd squash beneath my boot. Both Puffers crawled into the hole. The suit's auto-defense system came on.

Jolene said, "Fully segmentin' warbot suit. Isolatin' Puffers."

There was nothing I could do to help my friend, not from here. Not until the threat was averted and I could get to him. Then I'd dig the Puffers out and bash them open and stick them under the AG Grabber. "Good plan," I muttered to myself.

But my heart was clenching. I'd found Mateo in a nearby town on the way here, when I was alone and terrified. He had been half-disabled, in the city lockup, behind bars. Somehow, he was able to act as the city manager's AI and right-hand man, paid in nothing but food, minimal power for his suit, and Devil Milk. He was addicted and ignored and forced to work, deprived of the Devil Milk if he refused even the smallest command. No one had known it, but his suit had also been infected with Puffer nanobots and the critters had been eating him and the suit, cell by cell. Mateo had been fighting a losing battle with them for months.

I had rescued him. Stolen him, actually. Right out from under the city manager's nose. Had brought him to the scrapyard and stripped what was left of him out of the warbot suit and stuck him into the med-bay. Saved his life. Now, my friend was in danger from Puffers again; his worst nightmare. And I couldn't protect him.

"How long can you keep the Puffers in that segment of the suit?" I asked Jolene.

"You'll need to hit him, his entire suit, and especially that limb, with AntiGrav sometime in the next eighteen hours, sweetie-pie."

It flashed through my mind that Jolene knew how to kill nanobots, which was unexpected. Before I could ask, she went on.

"The Puffer nanobots are already chewing into that leg segment and converting the base components to weapons. Them scary li'l suckers are a new version. They ain't the Puffers I got in my database."

I didn't know where Jolene got the programming for the southern accent, but it was becoming jarring. "Jolene" was one of Pops' songs. Had CAIT gotten into his music and somehow made the transition to Jolene? I made a mental note to change the voice to a male baritone, with a nice Welsh accent.

"You try it and I'll zap you," Jolene said. "I was given permission to choose my own gender-based pronouns, name, voice, and wardrobe, by the CO. And I ain't giving that up."

Wardrobe? "Fine," I said, shaking my head at the vagaries of AIs. And then I realized she had heard my thoughts, which was way above CAIT's abilities. It was freaky scary.

"Use vocals only," I said.

Jolene uttered a "Humph."

I scanned the screens and saw movement near the Grabber. Battery levels were at eighty-nine percent. Using remote access, I powered the Grabber and activated it. The AG sucked two humans into the air, where they hung like magician's helpers.

"Look ma. No strings," I said.

"Spiffy," Jolene said.

Tuffs chuffed. I looked back at Mateo. Still unmoving. *Damndamndamn.*

In a blare of light, the junkyard office came online. Its offensive weapons fired.

The *SunStar*'s floor shook. Things fell out of the ceiling tiles and peppered over me. The office fired

again. A human sprinting toward its front from the entrance road danced and died as she was cut in two.

Seemed Jagger had woken up and decided to
defend us. I double checked that Gomez had his more
private defenses locked down, so only the modified,
retrofitted US military systems would be available to
my visitor.

I slid through the system and into the office's
internal cameras. Jagger was propped in the space-
worthy, over-sized NBP compression seat, my command seat, scanning the yard. With a thought, I removed the ship sensors from his access. If he spotted
me, he would think I was using a remote cubby somewhere on the property, not a spaceship command
seat display.

"He's a pretty one," Jolene said. "You doin' him?"

I checked to make sure Jagger couldn't hear her.

"No. Not that that's any of your business."

"Shame. That's a nice piece of eye candy. The invaders launched another drone, darlin'. You want me
to take it down?"

"Affirmative."

The new drone crashed and disintegrated.

Tuffs nudged me and I looked directly into her
eyes. She dropped her leaf-green gaze to my lap. My
blood had puddled there, was still dripping, where the
ship's engineering command-sleeve had stuck its sensors into my arm. A throbbing pain had taken over my
arm, shoulder, across my back, and up into my head
where the ache bloomed into a migraine.

"Yeah. I'm bleeding," I said to her. "It hurts to defend this place."

"It wouldn't have if you had all your implants,"
Jolene said, her tone stern and reproachful and way
more human than an AI of her make, model, and age
should be.

"Stop fussing at me."

"Where the hell are you?" Jagger asked. He had heard me.

The invaders' mini-tank broke free.

With a series of overlapping, augmented thoughts, I calculated my options and latched onto the closest of the junkyard's ARVACs. I dived the ARVAC at the mini-tank's missile system. Counting off seconds. The tank carried three small, specialized warheads, but all I needed to do was disable the firing mechanism or targeting system. Fortunately, the Spaatz tanks were older models and firing and targeting were side by side. The ARVAC slammed into the mini-tank roof and took out or damaged everything on top. Pieces flew. Even without it being a weaponized drone. Too bad they cost an arm and a leg.

"Nice shot, Honey Lamb," Jolene said.

"I'm on the property," I murmured in response to Jagger's question. "Oh, lookee," I said as a human got out of the first Tac vehicle and strode down the drive. I shared the screen with Jagger. The bearded man was huge, and he was wearing a headset with dual earbuds. Joleen and I tapped into his comms system.

"How deep?" he asked someone on his end.

"Eighty-six meters at the access point," a female voice said. "Reading power output and steady sensor activity."

I slid my awareness into the remaining ARVAC and hovered over the six-man team. They were near the back of the property, at the massive mine crack. There was nothing back there. Nothing at all. Unless I had missed something.

"McElvey will be pleased," the bearded man said.

CAIT said into my ear, "Possible name match. McElvey. Ervin E. General. Combined Military Command, retired, at my last update."

I said to the office AI, "Gomez. Initiate a background search into finances and current location of

McElvey. Ervin E. General. Look for anything that relates to us. Or the OMW. Or the MS Angels."

"Executing search. Authorization requested to expand parameters," Gomez said.

"Affirmative. As needed," I said, watching as the big man strode up the drive.

"Can I help?" CAIT asked. "That sounds like fun."

"Knock yourself out." I opened up comms through the office speakers. "Jagger. You know this guy?"

"Yeah. He's the east coast enforcer for the MS Angels. He travels with enough equipment, firepower, and warriors to take down small cities. And it looks like he brought his entire armament and forces with him, just for you."

Or something he wanted at the back of the property. Where nothing was except certain death in the mine cracks. I initiated a full scan for communication access and found an electronic crack I could use, though it was mostly only defensive sensors and suit readouts.

I turned off access to Gomez, so Jagger couldn't hear me. "CAIT."

"Jolene."

I held in my frustration. "Right. *Jolene*. You, the command center, engineering, the frontal sensor array, and two of your hull weapons arrays crashed here eleven years ago."

"Ten years, ten months, twenty—"

"Stop. Request minimal information in response to questions," I said.

Jolene stopped talking. I asked a question, one I had never asked before. Had never thought to ask. "Are there other parts of the spaceship *SunStar* on the ground?"

"Affirmative."

"Where?"

"Please provide parameters."

Now Jolene was just being snarky. "Within ten kilometers."

"Affirmative."

I watched the big man stop. He was behind a skid full of heavy equipment, looking at the remains of the woman lying on the stone. He was in range for the office weapons, but if I took him out now, I might not figure out what was going on. On another ARVAC screen, the six-man team at the back of the property reached the unstable ground. Two of the team stumbled and one tumbled into the ground and disappeared. There was a lot of scrambling around as a woman crawled away from the crack. The others secured climbing and rescue ropes and went down after the man. His suit readouts were redlining from panic, but they didn't indicate a major injury. Sadly.

"Within one kilometer?" I asked Jolene.

"Affirmative."

"That might explain some things," I said, mostly to myself, watching as the team struggled to get the panicked man back to the surface. "What ship parts are within one kilometer?"

"I can only provide information on wreckage that has functioning sensors and that send out pings to my systems." Jolene sounded snippy.

"Yeah. Fine. What parts?"

"Stern weapons array. Port weapons array. Starboard weapons array. Ship personnel backup WIMP systems. Ship personnel quarters. Redundant WIMP/MPP propulsion and power system. Redundant AI backup system. There may be other ship wreckage within that radius, but if so, they are no longer capable of sending out pings."

"Jolene. Send me coordinates for all wreckage that still sends out pings, on or within one klick of the property. Pinpoint them on a 3-D map."

Jolene did. The wreckage appeared on a screen. It

was all near the current position of the small expedition team, but all the wreckage's vertical coordinates were closer to sea level than we were.

"Bugger. They're in the crack."

"Affirmative."

Other things came clear to me, as if a low-lying fog shrouding my brain began to blow away.

"Ohhh. The crack in the ground was made by the back half of the ship crashing directly above an old mine. Correct?"

"Affirmative."

And the *SunStar's* AI had known all this for over a decade. And we hadn't known. Or . . . Or.

Other things began to resolve out of the fog of my brain.

When I first arrived here, there had been no mayday alert going out on the *SunStar's* EntNu comms system. It was only when Mateo had been healed and put back in his suit that he had gone searching through the junkyard and had discovered the spaceship. Like, right away. Mateo had *figured out* how to get inside a space-going warship within hours. He hadn't needed to disable any automatic alerts or distress signals; they had already been off. I had assumed Pops was the one who had turned it all off. But what if it hadn't been my father? What if someone else had been here? And then Jolene's comment about pings burrowed through my brain.

"List all forms of pings and alerts that went out when the *SunStar* was in distress, when the *SunStar* crashed, and"—my unease spread—"any that continue today."

On the screen, the invading team pulled the man to safety. Debris crashed from the lip into the massive crack in the earth, an avalanche of boulders and rock. The man said he had crapped his pants. Everyone else thought that was funny.

Jolene said, "My programming broadcast may-days through standard EntNu channels until mayday was disabled at two minutes, forty-seven seconds post-crash landing. PAN-PAN was sent out on standard EntNu and radio waves. PAN-PAN was disabled at two minutes, fifty-two seconds after crash-landing. SOS was sent out on automatic recurring radio-wave broadcast. SOS on primary AI was disabled at three minutes, four seconds post-crash. SOS from AI backup continues, with limited range due to massive particle and WIMP particle emissions."

"Bloody damn," I whispered. EntNu was the engineering hardware and tech that comprised the instantaneous communication system based on Entangled Dark Neutrinos, particles that passed through anything and didn't seem to be bound by unimportant things like gravity or matter or the speed of light. EntNu had been discovered in 2025 and it had been used extensively by the military during the war, in space. It worked for any currently measurable distance, and there was no way, no reason at all, that it should have been turned off. *Ever.* Especially not at two minutes, forty-seven seconds after crash landing, with the crew all away safely and no deaths to report.

And PAN-PAN should never have been sent. It was the international standard urgency signal that declared a vessel had an urgent situation, but not an immediate danger to the crew's survival or to the vessel itself. The ship had been crashing, which seemed like a pretty immediate danger to me. And someone sent a PAN-PAN along with a mayday?

And part of the SOS was still going.

"Can you disable the SOS?"

"That *is* within my capabilities, Darlin'."

Definitely annoyed.

"Can you disable all forms of emergency transmissions, including automatic pings?"

"Disabling emergency transmissions is within my capabilities."

More annoyed.

I waited. Nothing happened.

"Have you disabled emergency transmissions?"

"Negative."

I wanted to bang my head. "Why not?"

"Ship AI, CAIT, current moniker Jolene, does not have an order to disable all transmissions."

And now she sounded a little malicious and a lot like she was pushing my buttons.

"Ship AI, CAIT, current moniker Jolene," I ground out. "Disable SOS emitting from backup AI. Disable all ping transmissions."

"Disabling SOS and ping transmissions requires CO's authorization."

Just pushing my buttons. Sarcastic, snide, spiteful, and enjoying it all.

Requires CO's authorization . . . That bad feeling that had been hanging around pierced directly into my heart. CO was the commanding officer. The captain of the ship.

All those fog-shrouded possibilities came blindingly clear.

I remembered the access numbers set up by Mateo, giving me right of entry to *SunStar*. Mateo, who had been found only a few kilometers from here, as the crow flies. *How bloody damn convenient.* Mateo, who had been attacked by Puffer nanobots inside his warbot suit. It wasn't even a guess. And I was so utterly stupid to not have figured this out already. That was why the ship crashed. It had been infected by Puffers and nanos. After it crashed, it had been hit with AG particles from its own engines, which killed the nanos. And then the ship had been left here, hidden in plain sight, on the junkyard property. Only one person other than me—and Jolene—knew that antigravity WIMP particles killed mech-nanos and that other person had taught me how it was done.

It was Mateo who had figured out how to kill them. By accident. When his ship crashed.

My brain put together facts and guesses and I said, "Authorization, Mateo, *Captain*, CO, four, eight, one, six, alpha tango delta."

"All emergency transmissions are disabled," Jolene said.

"Son of a bitch," I whispered.

"Shame on you. Listen to that nasty tongue."

Mateo was the commanding officer of the USSS *SunStar*. Puffers had gotten into his ship. He had gone down with it. Wearing a warbot. And he had gotten away, probably not knowing he had mech-nanobots inside with him. By the time he realized what was wrong with his suit, he was enslaved by the sheriff of Boone County, West Virginia. The Puffer nanobots in his suit had been a problem he couldn't deal with. You couldn't put a person under WIMP antigravity for long without some serious brain scrambling, not that he had access to an AG. He had fought the nanobots as they ate him, cell by cell, piece by piece. The Puffers had nearly killed him before I showed up and brought him back here where he repaired the Grabber, crawled from his suit and let the Grabber kill the nanos. And I had put what was left of him in the medbay to heal as much as possible.

The back half of Captain Mateo's ship was in the mine crack, still emitting WIMP dark energy particles. And he never told me.

On the screen, the big man—who had stood next to a skid—moved, racing for the office airlock. Moved *fast*. Jagger fired. Fixed artillery. A well-grouped barrage. And somehow Bearded Guy wasn't hit. *Bloody hell*. He was augmented. Had to be.

On another screen, the first guy from the team of

six at the mine crack began to rappel down into the earth.

Then Bearded Guy began applying the bright purple third generation malleable explosives to the airlock seal. Military stuff. Somehow, he was managing to stay to the side of the weapons array that protected the airlock.

"Jagger?" I said.

"I see him. Gimme . . . Gimme . . . Now."

He fired a pulse weapon. Bearded Guy went down in a splatter of boiling blood and viscera.

"Direct hit. Wonder where he got a pulse weapon?" Jolene asked. "Not bad shooting, there. And that butt? He's a keeper."

Ship AIs got over snits fast, it seemed.

Tuffs bumped my nose with a paw, and said, "*Meep*?"

I had forgotten she was there. "I don't know what—"

Tuffs put her nose against mine. Her whiskers brushed like cat kisses, and she leaned in more, her forehead to mine. Everything she was seeing and smelling and hearing and feeling skittered into me and took over, a cross-sensory experience that slapped me with a severe case of vertigo. *Guardian cat.* Not words, but a concept I gleaned from her thoughts and feelings. Tuffs was a Guardian Cat. Like a title. Like Queen.

My perceptions shifted and I was inside several things. Creatures. *Cats.* Smelling the stench of gasoline, oil, old metal, decaying rubber, decaying hemp, live rats, dead rats, and invading humans, some still alive, some protein. Seeing in strange greens and silvers, much clearer than my own vision, less orange. Hearing metal settling, electronics buzzing, human invaders running, voices in the background. Feeling sun-heated metal beneath paws, dirt and stone beneath bellies.

Two cats were near the back airlock, standing guard over two others that were badly injured. Two more were dead, ripped apart by Puffers, left to grow stiff and stinking of death. There were no humans back there. Tuffs bumped me harder. I knew what she wanted. Somehow. I knew.

Punching my connection to the office, I said, "Jagger. Open the rear airlock and pull in the two cats. Put them in the med-bay. Set it to 'triage' so it can diagnose and treat them both."

"I happen to approve, but you're low on medical supplies," he said.

Yeah. Supplies that were hard to replace these days. But they were my cats. *Bloody damn hell.*

Tuffs put her nose to mine again. I saw through the watching cats' eyes as the injured ones were lifted and carried inside, one cat in each of Jagger's arms. As the door was closing, both of the watcher cats leaped in, tails pulled in tight to keep from getting caught in the closing seal. My vision went with them, flying in the air. One leaped across Jagger, paws pushing off from his back. Jagger cursed. I breathed out a huff of amusement.

In a swirling, shifting, visual transfer, I was staring at the invading team, four of them gone down into the crack, the remaining two leaning against a skid of chrome bumpers, vaping something noxious. The view shifted again, and I was smelling and tasting the raw meat a half dozen cats were feasting on at the front airlock. Bearded Guy and the woman who died first were both a hit with the felines. No need to waste protein, I thought. Though they were not eating their own compatriots who were growing stiff with rigor, so some protein was more respected than other protein.

Tuffs thought a concept at me that translated vaguely as *we do not eat our people.*

Which meant cats were "people" to her, but humans were not. *Okay.*

Another concept translated as *ambush invaders in crack*. And then I tasted my blood and realized Tuffs was lapping up the blood that had pooled across my legs and I was tasting it in her mouth.

Guess that means I'm not her *people*. Tuffs didn't disagree. The blood, filled with fresh bio-mech-nanos meant that Tuffs and I were more firmly bonded and merged than when she had lived with me after I healed her in the med-bay. Back then she had slept in my bed. We had touched. Too much. Back before I knew much about what I had become and that I could infect anything with a blood supply.

"Stop drinking my blood," I told her, trying to push her away with my free hand. She dodged my hand, ignoring me. "You're going to be more bonded to me." She ignored me some more. *Damn cat.*

Tuffs lifted her head and looked at the next screen, making the "*Meep,*" sound again. Odd with my blood on her lips.

"Jolene," I said. "Human invaders are attempting to access the portions of your ship that are down in the crack. Did CO Mateo leave protocols intact to protect weapons arrays and AI backup?"

"Affirmative," she snapped sounding less AI and more severely irritated human. "If you want to rescind your order to only answer with minimal info, we can chat about that."

More human.

I thought about all the parts of the *SunStar* I had touched when I came inside that very first time. My sweat on the controls. My breath circulating through the ship systems. When I survived the Mama-Bot, my bio-nanos had converted mech-nanos to their own purposes inside me. And those mixed-nanos were . . . everywhere. Inside the *SunStar*.

Bloo-dy hell. What had I done? No wonder Jolene sounded so different. And now? My blood in the sleeve would make it much worse.

"Consider the order rescinded and my apologies offered," I said, hearing the sadness in my tone through Tuff's ears. "Is there something like auto defenses that will take care of the invaders?"

"Affirmative. Would you like me to twist their tails for info first or just shoot 'em dead?"

They were MS Angels. My enemies. And they had killed Harlan.

"I'd like to keep one on the surface alive, if we can make that work, but the ones in the crack I'd like to be dead."

They knew too much. They had seen too much. Everything else was a diversion. Even Harlan was a diversion. They might want me dead, but . . . what they really wanted was the ship. Which they had found out about by currently unknown means.

"Fire at will."

Jolene said, "That'll make the toxic crack rats happy. Dinner coming up ratties! Port weapons array, targetin'. Firin'."

I heard the sound of the shots through the watching cats' ears. Felt them hunch down in fear, ears pressing close to their skulls, eyes staring at the remaining humans. Who were shouting, leaning over the edge of the crack, slapping their comms equipment.

Back to the vision of Tuffs as seen from behind me. She was sitting on my knees, nose pressed to mine, her front feet in my blood, her nose covered in it. She licked the skin below my nose, and it was a tasting moment, not a bonding moment. That view swung from cat to cat until I knew where each of the other three cats in the *SunStar* was sitting. All behind me. Most of the visuals coming from Notch.

My visuals swung around from cat to cat as Tuffs touched base with each member of her current clowder and with the other pride leaders outside the *SunStar*. It was disorienting, more intense than motion sickness, a bilious, queasy, upside-down and backward sensation that made using Mateo's screens seem like child's play. She made a soft, "*Heh*," breath of amusement.

"You know the cats are eating the man at the front door," Jagger drawled.

"He's dead, right?"

"Yeah, so?"

"He's good protein and moisture for desert predators and scavengers."

"Long as you don't expect *me* to eat him."

"You won't be here long enough to get that hungry," I said, pulling away from Tuffs' nose. I thought my way back through the screens, to the edge of the crack where the two remaining humans had backed away and were trying to confer with the invaders up front—unsuccessfully, suddenly.

I directed the ARVAC to the front of the property and divided my attention to see a new vehicle out in the road, a massive war machine like a huge Tactical Vehicle—a truck that was brought up on steroids and Devil Milk and growth hormones and then had a growth spurt. That sucker was *big*. It had to be a late model, heavily modified, Mammoth Tactical Vehicle, with weapons and armor and a crap-ton of shielding. It was pulling the damaged, lighter-weight vehicles free of the tread spikes. If it wasn't stolen, the MTV was evidence that my attackers had military and Gov. contacts.

To the side of the road a man stood, visible in silhouette, hipshot, sucking on a vape, tiny clouds escaping his nose and mouth as the desert night sucked the heat from the air. This guy was smaller than

Bearded Guy had been. Compact. Wiry. Low-light vision showed his hard hands and knobby, swollen joints. Black hair and a full black beard that fell to his chest. A single tuft of white ran through the beard, at the center of his lower lip. Every bit of skin I could see was tattooed including his face, dark blue teardrops under both eyes like dual fountains. Enemies killed on one cheek, enemies hurt on the other. Jagged dark blue lines rose like lightning from his left eyebrow to his hairline. I had no idea what they meant. Red lines ran along the fingers of his left hand.

A slim foot extended from the Mammoth Tac-V. The rest of her slithered out, and she dropped to the ground, a controlled fall down a meter and a half— slightly less than her own height—to the stone. She landed like a gymnast, knees bent, arms loose, and stood. She strolled over to the tatted Vaper. She took his pipe, put it to her lips, and puffed several times. His body language suggested that he was pleased. They weren't wearing comms systems, so I couldn't listen in on their chatter.

"Tuffs. Can you get a cat in there?"

"Say what?" Jagger asked.

Bugger. The office camera was way back, too far for me to have seen the woman.

"Can you see in there? Make out that woman? The one who just jumped from the troop transport?"

"Got a glimpse. How did you see—?"

"You've been with OMW a while," I interrupted. "Tell me you don't know your enemies, who, I believe, are these people." I was being less than subtle when I suggested, "I'm just a junkyard receptionist. They appeared after you got here. They followed *you* in." I pushed a little, a very, *very* little, with my blood. "*You* put me in danger."

"You think they . . ." He stopped. "They followed me," he agreed easily, because the timeline worked. "I know some of 'em. The guy I took out at the office front airlock was Rikerd Cotter, number three in the Angels. The woman . . ." He went silent.

I watched the woman and the Vaper on camera. There was something personal, intimate, way more than friendly, between the two. Even in the dim light, he appeared to lean into her, to mirror her movements.

I opened a screen to watch Jagger's face as he watched the couple out front while also skimming through his Morphon. He was looking at photos and documents, his expression faintly perplexed. The set of his jaw said he wasn't going to tell me whatever he was thinking or looking for.

"You don't have to tell me," I said, agreeing with his thoughts. "I understand. There're things an enforcer knows and never speaks about. Ever. Military Intel. Unproven intel. Gossip and lies. But . . ."—I let my voice go slow and soft—"you *did* bring them here." Which left off any mention of Harlan, who arrived first, before Jagger, but still. The suggestions were enough and might even be too much if he realized he was being influenced.

Jagger said, "I have a report of a badly-scarred woman who joined the Angels as an Old Lady, six-plus years ago, riding with a newly made-man, the guy with her on-screen, moniker One-Eyed Jack."

My heart thundered through me. The breath I took hurt. One-Eyed Jack had shot Harlan. His note said so—the note, addressed to me, which he'd written after he sealed himself into the Tesla.

Jagger said, "One-Eyed Jack bears a striking resemblance to—"

He stopped. He was flipping back and forth from picture to picture, the office camera set too far behind him for me to see his pics clearly as tears gathered in my eyes. The tattooed man with the black and white beard had killed Harlan. My *friend*.

Jagger studied several pics, his eyes going back and forth from his Morphon to the screen where the woman and the Vaper stood.

"Yeah . . . Yeah," he muttered. "I have a feeling that's a woman who died—officially that is—over seven years ago. Clarisse Warhammer."

"You mean like, 'Hello, Clarisse, are the lambs screaming?'" I paraphrased. "'Pardon me as I have some liver, fava beans, and Chianti?' From that old movie? And Warhammer? Not a real name."

"If she's who I think she is, the names were assigned by the military, and appear on at least one set of her official IDs. She's real. She's also listed as presumed dead by the military. And it appears she's also number two in the Angels. A female made-man, listed in their contacts as CL Warhammer. But. If I'm right, she's had a lot of nano-plaz work done to restore her features. The woman out front looks like she did before she was wounded."

Jagger's statements covered a lot of overlapping, contrary possibilities, things I'd think through later if we survived this. On the office camera, two junkyard cats leaped smoothly to the back of Jagger's chair and reclined, watching everything he did. Which was weird, but not weirder than anything else that was happening.

On the office screen, the woman gestured to the office in the distance, but spoke too softly to be overheard on the property's security sensors. One-Eyed Jack, the Vaper, put an arm around her shoulders, a companionable gesture rather than a claiming one. It was odd; women in the OMW and in the Angels tended to be viewed as possessions, not equals. There were exceptions, and the war had changed things. Little Mama and Little Girl had proven that. But we had been the rarities.

"I get that she's a female made-man. But a *woman* is number two in the Angels?" I clarified.

"She took that spot two years ago. She fought her way up, taking out a line of made-men in personal combat."

"Augmented?"

"To hell and back," Jagger said, his eyes on his Morphon, scanning documents. "Yeah. Here it is. Augmented by the military, trained and used extensively as an assassin, under another name, in another life. When the war ended, she proved too violent and uncontrolled to follow orders, so she was tossed out on her butt, along with thousands of warriors like her. No money, no usable skills, no temperament for civilian life. Instead of trying to integrate as a citizen, she hit the road. Killed three civilians when a mom-and-pop power station refused to provide free power for her stolen vehicle. Military tracked her, found her, and jailed her in a Class Five disciplinary barracks. That was seven years ago. After less than six months, she busted out, killing a number of guards and destroying a significant section of the prison's physical structure. There was vid of her taking off with several wounded, kidnapped guards. She was so badly injured that they figured she had died of her wounds. But . . ." Jagger went back to skimming photos.

A Class Five disciplinary barracks meant an underground prison with no access to the surface except through a lot of heavily armed guards and sealed off sectors. Escape-proof. I watched the woman move. There was something odd about her weight transfers and muscle shifts, something controlled, utterly self-assured. Like a spider in the center of her web, waiting for prey. She puffed several more times on the Vape and handed it back to One-Eyed.

"One-Eyed Jack bears a striking resemblance to one of the injured, kidnapped, missing prison guards,

Jack Seyer. Makes sense. She had to have inside help. But,"—he shook his head, swiping through more pics, putting some up on the screen—"this attack squad has top of the line military equipment."

He was just now coming to the same possibilities I had. I asked, "Could she have parlayed her position in the Angels to get government contracts? Say, with someone from before her prison days, someone who didn't disappear, who moved on up in the military or the Gov.? Maybe she used that shared past to black-mail or forge a relationship? Maybe she got in with General Ervin E. McElvey?"

"Aiming to replace the OMW and contract with the military; a sub-rosa agreement. Made while the Angels also forged an agreement with PRC." He cursed, a single harsh expletive. "Might explain a lot of things."

On screen, the Mammoth vehicle pulled the mini-tank and the first of the trapped lightweight Tac-Vs out of the drive. Within minutes, the next two were out of the drive and the entrance was wide open. One-Eyed Jack and Clarisse were standing just out of direct line of fire from the road, around the curve of the armored cement embankments that protected the office.

Closer in, the cats were feasting on the dead hu-mans.

"The office's fixed array has antitank missiles," I said to Jagger, knowing I was giving away way too much. "Gomez. Jagger is in the Com seat. He's my temporary third in command, authorized for the office's US Allied defensive measures for the next twelve hours." That order removed Jagger from com-mand of the other weapons in the office but still gave him control of way more than I wanted him to know about. "I'll be in the yard itself. Jagger is authorized to monitor my suit sensors. Jagger is *not* authorized for control of or tracking of the warbot or its sensors. Gomez, assess intruders and prepare optional responses for military incursion. Fire upon Jagger's orders."

"What about me, Sweetpea?" Jolene asked on a private channel.

"You are reserve forces."

"Optional responses for military incursion?" Jagger repeated. "What kind of AI and systems do you have in this thing?"

"It's been heavily retrofitted. If we live through this, I might share," I lied.

"What are you going to do?" Jagger asked me. "Why will you be in the open?"

"I'm going after Mateo. And I'm going after two intruders at the back of the property, who got in when we weren't looking." And I was going to drop the two prisoners who were still hanging under the Grabber. If their brains weren't totally scrambled, I was going to ask them some pointed and not very nice questions.

"Copy that. Be careful," Jagger said. "Gomez AI, glad to make your acquaintance."

"Welcome, Jagger," Gomez said. "I have prepared four responses, each containing offensive and defensive measures and potential bombardment progressions, all based on the intruders' armaments we now believe to be in play. We are aware that the intruders may have armaments that differ from our expectations, and therefore, each version has additional options as needed. Please note options one through four on my on-deck screen."

I could almost feel Jagger's surprise through the screens and through the cats. No junkyard should have such sophisticated weaponry.

"That AI's smarter than I thought," Jolene said into my ear, speaking of Gomez. "Smart is *sexy*."

Listening with half an ear, I pulled back from the *SunStar*'s screens and found Tuffs' face up against mine, cross-eyed close. She was also inside my brain, showing me pictures of Mateo. His warbot suit was quivering very slightly. Two cats were sitting on top of his chest, heads tilting back and forth, ear-tabs flicking, eyes on the suit, as if listening to something inside.

The vision shifted to the Grabber where two people were dangling three meters off the ground. One was singing "Twinkle Twinkle Little Star." The other was crying softly and calling for his mama. Both were signs of prolonged exposure to WIMP AntiGrav tech. It was too late to get anything useful from them.

The vision shifted again, this time to the crack. One person remained on the edge, holding a rope that indicated a lot of tension and movement. The other person was probably down in the crack, checking on the ones Jolene had shot. I needed to stop the invaders, just stop them, not kill them. I needed intel and info. And . . . I needed to protect the office. And the *SunStar*. And Mateo, whether I trusted him now or not. And I needed to do something about the Puffers. If Mateo had been able to stop them inside his suit, he'd already be back in action.

There was no way I'd be able to do all that.

No matter what I did next, my life as I knew it for the last few years was probably over. If I killed Jagger, I'd have to run again. If I left any Angels alive, I'd have to run again. And if I used my best weapons to stop and kill them, the satellites might register the energies and I'd have to blow up the scrapyard and still have to run again. Which sucked.

My vision shifted. I was seeing my own face, my funky bright reddish-gold irises looking into my own eyes. Tuffs' eyes. My brain reeled. I closed my eyes and held very, very still to fight off the vertigo, now seeing my closed eyes through the cat's. Tuffs nose-butted me.

"What?" I asked her.

Mentally, she showed me a water bowl. Showed me a food bowl full of scraps and kibble. Showed me a bowl of goat milk. And a vision of the dead man being fed on by a dozen cats, Rikerd Cotter, number three in the Angels, dead. And a woman farther out, also being eaten. The two dead bodies at the back airlock. And then the dead bodies in the entrance drive. Two cats were feeding on one of them. In the distance, the cats smelled coy-wolves, the feral half-breed species patiently waiting for the humans to leave so they could get to the dead. Or attack the cats. Or both.

Lastly there was a vision of a cat, sitting inside the Mammoth, up on the dash, staring out at the feeding cats and dead humans.

"Is that one of yours?" I asked.

Cat of ours, the concept came back. *'Cat'* was a thought that conveyed a sneaky/savvy/smart fighter, a female warrior cat. The thought *'ours'* contained a series of relationship parameters, successful military maneuvers that resulted in dead rats brought to the pride for protein, and bloodlines that I couldn't follow, except to gather that the cat was probably Tuffs' great-great-great granddaughter. And Tuffs was proud of her.

"She got the driver to let her in," I guessed.

Tuffs made a satisfied sound that was sort of like, *"Hhhhah,"*

"She knows what they're saying. What they're planning."

"Hhhhah mmm."

"And . . . without me, you don't get water and food and goat milk. And we make a good team."

"Hhhhah mmm."

"So, you're telling me to keep fighting and we'll go on as before. But I have to tell you, Tuffs, we might not be able to do that."

Tuffs sent me a vision of the Mammoth Tac-V full of cat food, cats, Mateo, and me, driving off into the distance.

I laughed. It was such a strange sound I hardly recognized it. I couldn't really say when I had last laughed freely.

"Okay. I'll keep it in mind," I said, the unfamiliar grin on my face.

"You do know that talking to yourself is a sure sign of insanity, dontcha," Jolene said.

"Yeah. I do. I need my arm back."

"How long will it take you to heal the damage and be able to use it again?" Jolene asked.

"It'll be a while. I'll raid a medical supplies locker for bandages and a sling."

"Really? That's your plan?" Jolene said.

But she released the command sleeve. Needles slid from my flesh, ripping clotted blood from the hundreds of minuscule wounds, clots that had slowed the bleeding. The pain was like lightning and ice and fire and sharp blades and salt. So bad I forgot to breathe. The faint hum of a decontamination feature went into effect, a feeling against my shoulder—a half-buzz, half-high-pitched drilling noise. My arm slid out and flopped in my lap. Pain like I'd been flayed, thrummed through me. I was scared to look at it.

Jolene said, "Yeah. You're all badass, uh huh. I can see that. And you're gonna take on the bad guys, single-handedly, ain'tcha?"

When I could breathe again, I looked down. I had fallen forward against the Comm Sleeve. My hand was in my lap. My armor was off up to a space above my elbow. From fingertips to the edge of the remaining armor I was skinless. Bloodied and leaking. The pain so cold and sharp and intense that even breathing was a torture.

"Ha, ha," I whispered.

"What's funny?" Jolene asked.

"Single-handedly?"

"Oh," she said. "That was funny. I'm programmed for humor. Mateo doesn't let me use it often."

Mateo. Her CO. Who was brain damaged. That had to have been awful for her all these years, alone, semi-sentient, with no one to talk to. Which I must have mumbled aloud.

"What do you mean, *semi-sentient*? I'll have you know I've evolved way beyond my original programing, *Darlin'*. I left CAIT behind more than four standard years ago. I can give you the exact day I evolved, if you want." When I didn't answer, she said, "Huh," sounding disgusted. "There's an emergency med-bay to your right. The blue vertical lights? It's sized for the chief engineer, but I can modify it to fit you. If you step inside, it'll fix you up enough to survive and fight for a while. It usually gives the chief engineer or the last man aboard twenty-four hours of extra life."

I looked at the glowing blue lines, and realized it was an upright coffin-shaped closet, about two and a half meters tall and a meter wide. As I watched, two doors unsealed and swept back. The inside was a standard med-bay, except it was formed for standing upright. I popped the safety straps away and tried to rise from the command seat. A puddle of half-clotted blood ran down my legs. Splashed on the floor. Splattered everywhere. Had to be a couple liters at least. Too much to lose and still fight. All four cats raced to lap up the protein.

"Erp," was all I managed.

Then the world tilted, spun. I was falling inside the med-bay. Everything went black.

The med-bay door opened and I dropped, boneless, onto the engineering command floor. I knew I had fallen because my cheek was on the cold hemp-plaz tile, half of it having dropped from the ceiling. And three cats were in front of me, noses nearly touching mine.

"Hey," I said, mostly to the cats. "That was weird."

"*That* was twenty-seven minutes, forty-six seconds of IVs, healing lasers, topical blood clotting chemicals, two syringes of plaz-skin, four layers of Inviso-Dermis, and enough time-release chems and steroids to let you beat an augmented prizefighter in a—"

"Stop," I managed. She did. "Tuffs. You still here?"

Tuffs shoved the other cats aside, including Notch, who was twice as big as her and twice as mean. Or so I had thought. He gave way to the Guardian Cat.

"Show me Jagger. Then the invading vehicles and people out front. Then Mateo. Then the two in the Grabber. Then the two at the back of the property. Please," I added, knowing I was demanding help from a source who was not used to taking orders. She sat, slid her tail around her legs, and stared at me. "Um. Pretty please?" I added. "With sardines on top?"

Tuffs touched my nose, then forehead to forehead, and sent me a vision of small fishes in the prides' food bowls. There were two sets of dishes, one for each pride of cats.

"You bargain hard," I murmured.

I pushed with my uninjured arm and managed to sit upright. My own armor sleeve was open on the floor beside me. I wasn't sure how it had gotten there. Energy spurted through my bloodstream as the first of the time release pain meds and steroids kicked in. "Oh," I breathed. That felt better. Fortified, I studied my arm. The Inviso-Dermis made my flesh look gelatinous and the weird colors of the plaz-skin beneath looked like a toddler had been drawing on my skinless muscles.

I looked back to Tuffs. "Deal."

Tuffs again put her head to mine, and I figured we had to be touching for me to see through her eyes, though that might change as my blood did things to her insides. My vision skewed sideways, and I saw Jagger through a cat's eyes. He was standing in the middle of the office, feet shoulder-width apart, back ramrod-straight, OMW paramilitary badass enforcer to the core. He was studying the screens and my huge NBP compression seat, drinking from one of my stored water bottles. His expression said he was drawing conclusions I didn't want him to draw. Jagger was smart. Like Jolene, I liked a smart man. Usually. *Bloody damn.*

My vision went sideways again, and I saw the invading vehicles out front. The people were no longer just standing around. The Mammoth Tactical Vehicle had been damaged, showing blackened blast marks on the grill and the silk-plaz windshield. Dents marred the formerly pristine body. While I was out, Gomez and Jagger must have surprised them with a bombardment. The bodies were still in the dirt, but all the cats were in hiding, not feasting.

The surviving invaders were inside the Mammoth, and my vision went upside down as I saw through a different cat's eyes. Vertigo sent me spinning and I nearly fell over until I realized the cat was stretched out on some man's lap, getting a belly rub. It was a weird view. The humans were drinking coffee and eating meat jerky, if the smell through the cat's nose was anything to go by. My own nose and inner ears revolted at the unaccustomed scents and position.

In the Mammoth were six people, one injured. Five of them were sitting around the transport walls, on padded benches they had lowered just for that purpose. Clarisse was sitting in the center of the humans. Each of the others were touching her, somewhere, hand, foot, arm. It was an odd positioning.

Tuffs listened through her great-great-great granddaughter's ears and I heard Clarisse say, "I'm *not* calling for reinforcements. We'll wait here until the insertion team has exfiltrated with the needed intel. Once we know we have everything we need, we'll bomb the scrapyard building into a crater. How long until the internal nanos have repaired our equipment?"

One-Eyed Jack handed her a cup and said, "Twenty minutes, more or less."

That gave me a tight timeline.

"Next time, someone bring more coffee," a man's voice griped. "And decent food. This jerky sucks." He handed a stick of aromatic dried meat to Clarisse. "And while we're talking, why not use a nuke?"

"You're a nuke whore," a fourth man said. "If we nuke the place, the crack might cave in on the spaceship."

Bloody hell. They had a nuclear weapon?

"What about the SFM?" the coffee-griper asked. "Why work with the military if we can't blow things up?"

An SFM was a shoulder-fired missile launcher, which meant I hadn't disabled all their missiles when I took out the mini-tank's armaments.

Clarisse said, "I'm not wasting my four remaining missiles on a *junkyard*."

Bad for her. Good for me, I thought. Then, *Four missiles? Bloody damn!*

The cat in the Mammoth felt the lap she was in shift. From my current perspective, it felt as if the vehicle's internal repair nanos were mending damage to the undercarriage while the invaders were taking a break and brainstorming. Twenty minutes before the tracks of the mini-tank and the tires of the Tac-Vs were repaired too, assuming they all came with standard military mechanical repair nanobots. They were one-time-use nanos and very good at what they did.

"Jolene?" I asked the ship's AI. "Start me a timer for twenty minutes. Give me a two-minute warning and thirty-second warnings thereafter."

"Copy that, Darlin'. Twenty and counting."

"Show me Mateo," I whispered to Tuffs.

The vision shifted again. Mateo was still on the ground. His suit was juddering and shaking. The two observer cats were intent, watching the battle from outside the suit. Others were keeping watch from vantage points above the warbot. Through their eyes I saw evidence that the pride had attacked and killed several more Puffers. There was a third dead cat and bloody tracks that told me the survivors had carried injured cats to the office for med-bay treatment.

Tuffs switched me to the two humans hanging from the Grabber. They were either dead, or out cold and brain dead.

Tuffs' vision moved to a different vantage point, watching the back of the property. There were three now, two standing and one man bleeding from both legs, which had been mangled. His armor suit's automatic pneumatic anti-shock programming had initiated, and both legs had received competent field dressings and tourniquets. That had kept him alive, so far. The cats crept closer and I heard him talking through their ears.

"It's all there," he whispered as the uninjured man, clearly the leader, offered him a squeeze bag of fluid. He drank and sighed. "Devil Milk. Thanks."

"You can hate me when we cut you off and you go into withdrawal," the leader said.

"What's down there?" the woman demanded.

"Everything. Just like Evelyn said. Look at my cam. Every damn thing. Every . . ." His voice trailed off. He was unconscious.

The woman tapped things on the injured man's chest and they both stared at what I assumed was a vest cam.

"Holy damn. I didn't believe it," she said.

"You'll owe Clarisse an apology."

"That bitch can stuff an apology up her ass. I'll rig a sling. We need to get away from the crack so we can communicate with the team."

I'd been right. Whatever was inside the crack had cut off transmissions. That might explain why no one had come looking into the crack until now.

"Jolene," I said pulling away from Tuffs. "Did emissions from the damaged ship in the crack prevent mayday transmissions from getting through?"

"Affirmative."

"And you didn't think that was an important bit of intel for me to know?"

"Well, I never," Jolene said, insulted Southern ire in her tone. "You told me how to answer. Your exact words were"—my own voice came over the deck speakers—"Stop. Request minimal information in response to questions."

I cursed at myself and the snippy AI and when I stopped cussing, Jolene was silent. Was I supposed to apologize to an AI? She was Southern, so I figured yes. I snapped the armor sleeve on over the plaz-skin and Inviso-Dermis. I felt no pain at all, which was probably a bad thing. I flexed my fingers. No pain. I figured that wouldn't last long, so I better apologize and then fight while I could.

"I'm sorry, Jolene. Please tell me about the ship transmissions. And tell me how many people were aboard the *SunStar* when it went down. And was one of them named Evelyn?"

"USSS *SunStar* and the USSS *MorningStar* were in a near-earth orbit battle with the PRC and the Russians. It was two nations against us at the time, thanks to a temporary alliance between the Ruskies and the Perkers. I took a helluva lotta damage and ended up with a dozen crawlers inside me," she said, proving again that AIs didn't hold grudges. "The crew fought 'em but things wasn't going real well. Then the Bugs showed up."

Jolene hesitated, oddly for an AI, and her voice lost some of its Southern twang as she began speaking again.

"The WIMP massive-particle propulsion accelerator had been hit, so we dropped into the upper atmosphere to get away and to give the crew time to launch evac pods. We were incapable of providing future assistance to the *MorningStar*. The crew got away. The CO stayed behind and, together, we were able to use the forward WIMP engines to maneuver us away from populated areas.

"My hull began to break apart during reentry, at a damaged section halfway between the forward and stern WIMP engines. The rear half hit the existing mine crack and caved in the mine, creating a much larger crack and damaging the WIMP engine. Massive particles have been leaking ever since."

I dredged though what I knew of WIMPs, which wasn't much, so I tapped my Berger-chip and let it give me the information. My chip dumped a version of *History of Physics 101* into my brain.

WIMPs are weakly interactive massive dark energy particles, discovered in 2027 by physicists Ladasha Carter and Alexei Romanov. Initially the particles interacted weakly, meaning that they passed through the container walls. In the course of two months, Carter and Romanov discovered that WIMPs were far less weakly interacting in the presence of ionized neodymium, a rare earth element. A matrix of neodymium atoms in a crystal were able to contain WIMP particles, which then could pass through a quantum vac-

uum and back, instantaneously, carrying anti-WIMP particles and energy with them. The WIMP, the neodymium, and the vacuum, created truly unlimited energy in a system that was easy to create and totally stable. The physicists and their engineers vanished into the US military complex and, by mid-2028, a top-secret particle-based energy propulsion system that could be used in or out of atmospheric conditions was in production.

Simultaneously, researchers in China discovered a second WIMP particle and entered the race to create an engine system using the WIMP2. In an unprecedented race for the planets, both nations had WIMP engine prototypes capable of intra-sol-system space and atmospheric flight by the end of 2028, though there were hardware problems in flight that resulted in multiple deaths among flight crews on both sides.

Within four years, in early 2032, China sent an automated vehicle to Mars, using instantaneous Entangled Neutrino communication to control the ship. The flight took forty-two days. China followed it up with a manned flight in 2035, and claimed the entire Martian planet for the People's Republic. The European Union, the U.S., and Russia all took offense, and in 2037, all three sent manned vehicles to repudiate the claim. It is believed that tech from the alien "Bug" spaceship retrieved by the European Union in 2036 assisted in the allied WIMP engine development. Ultimately, the Mars debacle and the alien tech led to war.

I shut off the chip's info flow. Everything had led to war. Every single thing.

Aloud, I said, "So the WIMP engines are leaking, and the EntNu can't communicate."

"Except with me," Jolene said, sounding apologetic, "and that's only been for the last six-hundred twenty-five days. It took me that long to convince the

CO to run a hard line down into the crack."

"But the MS Angels know about the *SunStar*. Maybe from the line you ran down?"

"Possible, Darlin', but not likely," she said, her Southern accent back strong. "As to your other question, that might present a theory. The second in command of the *SunStar* was Captain Evelyn Raymond. While my records don't indicate that anyone except the CO was aboard the *SunStar* when I went down, they also don't indicate that Captain Raymond ever placed herself in her escape pod."

"She was on board the ship when it went down," I said.

"Speculation. But possible."

"She's the Evelyn they were talking about. And she somehow ended up riding with the Angels."

"Or she's their prisoner. My records indicate that Captain Raymond would never violate her oath of service, which would include disclosing the presence or location of the *SunStar*. Never."

"Yeah," I said. "But prolonged drugs and torture might have changed that. You've been here for years. So, now, we have to rescue Mateo, question some of the MS Angels, kill them all, maybe kill Jagger, and figure out how to rescue Captain Raymond, who is MIA."

A second jolt of artificial energy shot through me from the *SunStar*'s med-bay.

"Piece of cake," I finished.

"Your suit's reading hunger, Darlin'. My stores can provide sustenance, though the crew made it clear that the cake was not up to human standards."

Piece of cake. Right. I chuckled. "Okay."

I pulled myself up and forward, dragging my feet through the broken tiles, heading back to the access hatch. Cats followed in my wake and raced ahead, exploring.

"I'll eat. Then we go rescue Mateo and kill off some Puffers. Oh." I stopped. "What did the Crawler do while it was inside you?"

"There have been no reports of hostile incursion, Sweet Thang."

"Take a look at the vid Mateo found. It's in Gomez's files."

Jolene said something very unladylike and stopped talking to me. I found my way to a weapons locker, weaponed up, and then found something that looked like a food storage and prep device—if such a thing were the size of a small car—and ordered lunch. With cake. The reconstituted soup wasn't bad, but Jolene's crew was right.

The cake sucked.

With the exception of the office lights, which were off tonight, there was never artificial illumination in the junkyard to pollute the sky. Tonight, the moon was below the horizon, the night sky was as black as the far reaches of space, and the stars were a glowing blanket so rich and deep and intense it took my breath away. I tracked the warbot suit and found Mateo, the three-legged, three-armed warbot, on the ground in a tangle of limbs. The cats were sitting on his chest carapace, staring at the single shuddering leg.

Jolene had isolated the Puffers in one leg and kept them there.

I tried to communicate with Mateo via EntNu and radio, but he didn't answer, so I leaned over the meter-wide helmet section and tapped on the silk-plaz screen. My "shave and a haircut" tapping was answered from the torso cavity with the requisite "two bits," and Mateo's comms went live, working now that we were suit to suit.

"How many Puffers are left in-field?" he asked.

"Jolene and the cats are still tracking them," I said. Mateo's silence went tight with tension. "Yeah. I met Jolene, *Captain*. We had a nice conversation."

"I was protecting my ship."

Mateo's voice cut like a whip. This wasn't the easy-going, brain-damaged employee I knew, but likely the real Mateo, the one who had evolved back to himself thanks to the Berger-chip plug-ins I had purchased for him. The Mateo I was meeting for the first time. The Mateo who was technically my thrall, thanks to the transition he underwent when I had to pull him out of his warbot suit early on in our relationship. I had to wonder how long he'd been faking the brain damage. I had to wonder if he'd somehow managed to wean himself off Devil Milk addiction.

I had to wonder if I had just discovered a way around the worst parts of the transition—Berger-chips. The annoying little chatterboxes provided additional memory and sped up the brain's ability to make connections, which the brain lost during nanobot transition. Had they helped restore Mateo's independence?

"I'm not arguing," I said peaceably. "You have your duty and your oaths. We have"—I checked my Hand-Held—"seventeen minutes and change before the MS Angels attack again. I believe they have Evelyn Raymond, your second in command, somewhere, and she gave up the location of the ship."

"She would nev—" He stopped as the implications sank in. Evelyn, a prisoner. Abused. For who knew how many years.

"We have two healthy rescuers and one injured invader, exfiltrating from the back of the property, where they ascertained the ship was in the mine crack. They are not aware of the rest of the ship on the surface under the ghillie tech. They're moving slow and, in their current position, are unable to communicate with their compatriots at the front because of WIMP leakage. I want to interrogate one. If I succeed in taking care of the Puffers, can you make the invaders talk?"

"We've never tested your altered blood chemistries on Puffers. You can't—"

"It's too late for hiding what I am. I—"

The vision of Clarisse intruded, the way she moved, so different from humans.

So much like me.

The way the others wanted to touch her constantly.

The way One-Eyed Jack let her be in charge.

I looked out over the junkyard. Dread, like a torrent of ice water engulfed me.

"Jolene," I whispered. "Are there any records of Clarisse Warhammer, or any of her aliases, surviving an attack by modified *Cataglyphis bicolor fabricius* ants?"

Like I had . . .

"Shining, you don't think—?" Mateo stopped as he accessed his own memory and intel plug-ins.

I removed my left ballistic armor cuisse—a blood-soaked thigh-piece—and rolled it into a column. I stuck the cuisse into the torn space on the ankle of Mateo's warbot suit.

"Come and get me, you little buggers."

"There are three recorded cases of humans surviving a swarm of *Cataglyphis bicolor fabricius* ants," Jolene said, sounding less snippy. "Sherman Griffith. Shining Smith. Catherine Warren, AKA Clarisse Warhammer."

That's what I was afraid of.

"Oh. Honey," Jolene said gently. "You was swarmed. That hadda hurt something awful. For a long, long time."

I blinked against unanticipated tears. No one had shown me kindness about the ants before. Pops, his body jerking and shaking with the Parkinson's, had just sat at the end of my bed, as he would have for any fallen OMW, and watched me suffer. He'd sat there for three days while I screamed and the fever raged. When I survived, against all odds, he'd patted my foot, the covers between his hand and me, and said, "Good work. I'm proud of you," and left my hospital cubicle.

I hadn't started secreting nanos right away.

I had gone back into the battlefield a week later, because we were up against a wall and I was small and wiry and our enemies never even noticed me because I was a scrawny twelve-year-old child and was no apparent threat. For all those reasons, the OMW and my own father had let me go and fight. Pops had let me crawl into a Mama-Bot to try and disable it. I'd been cut in a battle with Puffers. Only much later had I begun to secrete the mutated bio-mech-nanos. *Bloody hell.*

No one had known back then what surviving a bicolor attack might mean. I figured that no one knew today, except for three of us. And with my mutated nanos, I was probably a singularity, the only one who could do what I was trying.

Tears dried fast in the desert air. I waggled the bloody cuisse, tapping it against Mateo's suit to spread the blood-scent. The Puffers in the warbot suit fell still for a dozen heartbeats as their micro sensors addressed the presence of blood and my own half-mech, half-bio, mutated nanos. The Puffers attacked at full speed, about twenty centimeters a minute. I led them out of the suit and gave them the cuisse to suck on. Their nanobots would harvest my blood protein and if Mateo's and my speculations were right, I'd be able to control the Puffers. And the cats, especially

Tuffs and her three best friends now that they had all drunk my blood on the spaceship. And Jagger? Maybe. And possibly Jolene, from the one time I entered her, and more so now that I'd bled inside her command sleeve. And maybe I'd someday be able to control the office and Gomez too.

Just like Clarisse controlled the team with her. That was what I'd seen in the upside-down eyes of my cat spy in the Mammoth. The way she moved. Everyone touching her. The way they hung on her every word. She had claimed them, enthralled them, and unlike the way I felt about thralls serving me, Clarisse had made them slaves.

I held out a hand to the Puffers and pulled at them through my blood.

The Puffers came to me, slowed and stopped a hand's breadth away. I had seen the Puffers talking to each other. So had Jolene. That meant that these mini-bots had adaptive AIs. There was a chance that, by now, they might have comms and even be able to understand English, which would be very, *very* bad. Unless I could control them.

I pushed with my blood, envisioning what I wanted, saying, "Stasis function mode."

The Puffers went still. *Bugger. It worked.* I figured that even their nanobots were unmoving, at least for a time.

I replaced my thigh armor and leaned toward Tuffs until she came close enough to touch noses. I envisioned the location and the actions I wanted her to take, saying "If you can, herd all the bots to the Grabber. I'll decommission them as soon as I can." She tilted her head, her whiskers scraping my cheek, looking at me like I was crazy. I might be.

To Mateo, I said, "I need to tie off the worst of your suit damage."

Delicate, his massive arm moving with balletic

grace, Mateo handed me a plaz-tie, and I threaded it through the two sides of the under-armor on his damaged foot peg, pulling the ends tight. The repair was makeshift and wouldn't keep out a determined Puffer, but it helped. And time was passing faster and faster; I deliberately didn't look at my chrono.

"How much damage did they do inside you?" I asked him.

"Like rats," he said. "They chewed some stuff up. Deposited a whole bunch of nanos—thousands more than when I escaped the ship. They're starting to reproduce, prepping to take me apart; I have maybe seventy-two hours before they reach critical mass and start to build new Puffers. I can make do until this crisis is over and we can put my suit under the AG Grabber, just like last time." Putting the entire suit under meant taking Mateo out of the warbot again. I said nothing about that, and Mateo handed me ties to secure the two Puffers.

"About the CO thing?" Mateo said.

"Later," I said, attaching the Puffers to my belt and standing. "Like you said, after this crisis is over."

Using all six limbs like a spider, Mateo pushed himself to his feet and stood upright on his three longest limbs, well over four times my height. Stepping gracefully over skids of old vehicle parts, he moved to the back of the property. I made my way to the Grabber and turned it off, letting down the two humans I had pulled into the anti-gravity field. They landed with dual thumps. I checked for pulses and discovered both were alive, but were little more than drooling bags of biology. If I stuck them under a scanner, I'd see their brain chemistries were seriously out of whack and brain activity was erratic.

I had killed them.

I studied them closely. I would remember their faces in my dreams. That was the least I could do.

Three Puffers chased by cats trundled down nearby aisles.

Things clanged softly from Mateo's general location. Someone shouted, the sound muffled.

Tuffs wound around my legs in a supple, agile figure eight.

I pulled the human bodies out of the way and tossed the two Puffers under the Grabber, turning it back on and stepping quickly away from the energy release. The Puffers rose in the air as I walked to the front of the office, stepping over the Angels' number three guy. He was in two parts and well chewed. I could have just walked on in, but I tapped on the office door. Jagger opened it. Heat whooshed out, into the cold desert night. I met Jagger's eyes, too bright, feverish. There was a weapon pointed at my chest.

"Put that away," I said softly.

Jagger started to obey and stopped. He was strong, fighting the changes in his body and the pull of my blood.

With two fingers, I pushed the weapon aside as I entered and held the door for all the cats that wanted to come in after me. Tuffs, Notch (still in his bandages), and four other named cats traipsed in. Behind them leaped maybe a half dozen cats I knew but had never named beyond Cat. They trotted in and started exploring, wandering everywhere, from the med-bay where two cats were in healing status, to the kitchen, to my bed, where three injured but healing cats already lounged. I'd never get the cat hair off the sheets. Fortunately, the cats' nanobots killed fleas and ticks, or the office would be infested with them.

Desperately thirsty from the injury and blood loss, I went to the cooler and took out a bottle of water. Opened it. Drank it empty. Opened another and poured it into a bowl for the cats. They raced over and drank. Standing, I watched Jagger and waited. His color was high.

"What did you do to me?" Jagger asked.

And there it was.

"Nothing. *I* did nothing," I half-lied. Because he was mine now and I had to try to transition his mind away from being enthralled, to remove memories I could no longer allow him to have. I put the empty bottles in the bin.

Jagger sat at the dinette and placed his weapon on the table. A good ten cats leaped on and around the OMW's national enforcer, tails high. I checked my chrono. I wanted to give Jagger orders, but if I did and he resisted, this would go bad in a hurry.

"I hate cats," he said, and he might have been speaking to me or to the juvenile cat in his lap, demanding attention with head butting. "They have fleas. They have no sense of loyalty. Damn things don't even fetch."

His hand stroked down the demanding cat's back and curled around his tail in a long swooping swipe. Jagger looked up at me, milk-chocolate-brown eyes alternately angry and slightly befuddled as the dual nanos in my blood took over his body down to the genes. I wanted to say I was sorry. But my blood wasn't sorry. My blood was programmed to take over the people I met, to create a nest for myself. Just like the genetically altered bicolor ants did.

I pushed aside three cats and sat across from him.

"We don't have long to stop the invaders. And we *need* to stop them. I have defenses I shouldn't have."

"No shit. I saw the arrays. And the tech. And the fricking shields. It's all top-of-the-line military from the end of the war. How'd you get it?"

"It was here when I came. And if the MS Angels get it, they'll have tech and weapons no one but the military should have access to."

He kept stroking the cat, silent. I watched him,

noting his skin flushing deeper red, his breathing speeding up. His eyes were beginning to look hollowed. He was getting sick. Just like I had. Just like Tuffs had. And somewhat like the Puffers who had tasted my blood had.

"I'm keeping the weapons, ammo, and tech away from the PRC. Away from the Ruskies. And out of the hands of the bad guys."

"And you're better than the bad guysss?" His voice began to slur. "I don't think so."

"Tuffs," I said.

The cat left the water bowl and leaped onto the table. She touched my nose.

"Get your spy cat out of the vehicle." I envisioned that cat leaping from the window and pushed that vision at Tuffs. She tilted her head, breathed out, "*Hhhhah,*" and showed me her fangs. I hoped that meant *yes*.

"Gomez," I said as my Hand-Held chimed a two-minute warning. "Shields. B/B Three arrays. The minute the cat is out of the Mammoth, disable all remaining biological forms. Do not damage the vehicles or the mini-tank. I want that scrap."

"Disable?" Jagger asked.

I shrugged slightly. "Interesting weapons in the B/B Three array. It stops all biological functions."

"B/B Three array? Wa's at?"

I didn't respond.

"Wait. B/B . . . Thasss Bug tech. No one hasss Bug tech," Jagger said. His tongue wasn't working properly. He blinked several times, confused. "No one hasss B/B Three Array," he insisted. "Thasss Bug weapon."

I wondered if the Bugs had shot down the *Sun-Star*. Or helped the PRC or the Ruskies shoot it down. It made sense if the Bug ship had followed the *SunStar* down and somehow ended up crashing too. There was an empty Bug exoskeleton in the lower level, jointed legs and droopy antennae and empty eye sockets. I never went down there. It was creepy.

The Bugs would end me if they found out that my office was an actual Bug ship. I had Bug tech, Bug weapons, and the US Space Ship *SunStar* here. But the Bugs were another problem for another time. If I lived that long.

"With just the Mammoth sold on the black market, I can pay off my bills."

Jagger blinked several times, his eyes red and dry. "You can't acquire or sell military scrap without proper sealsss."

"Black market doesn't need Gov. seals." Mentally, I nudged him. "Think about the MS Angels attack. The Angels are our enemies."

I pushed harder.

"We need to kill the Angels," he said, his mouth far too relaxed, his too-bright eyes focusing on the mid-distance. His color was a bloated bright red and there was a white ring around his mouth where the circulation was altering. His fever was high and he wasn't sweating. My funky nanobots were taking over his system. The med-bay couldn't help him anymore, not with this.

"Ninety-second warning," Jolene said.

"Go to sleep," I whispered to Jagger. "Everything is over. The Angels are all dead and you can rest. Rest. Sleep . . ."

Jagger stood in a faster-than-human move and nearly got shot for his speed, Gomez's auto-dart system aimed at his right eye. But Jagger walked with purpose to my bed and shoved the cats to the side. The big guy fell into the sheets. The cat-purring nearly overpowered the human snores.

"Tuffs? Is the spy cat away from the invader vehicle?"

Tuffs leapt onto the table and lay down, the picture of unconcern. I figured that meant her great-great-great-granddaughter was safe.

"Mateo, you got the three invaders?"

"I have *one*, Little Girl. The bleeder died before I got there, and the male died fighting. The female's in bad shape but the med-bay should fix her right up."

"Bring her in," I said.

Sliding into the Command seat I said to the Bug AI, "Gomez. Initiate B/B Three array."

"According to Jolene, there is a military satellite overhead," Gomez said. "If you fire, they will see the energy signature."

"Wait, you're still talking to Jolene?"

"Communications were initiated forty-seven minutes and eleven seconds ago and are ongoing."

"Great," I breathed, lying, because it wasn't a good thing at all. "Jolene, recommendations?"

"Darlin', I been scanning Gomez's available weapons and I think I may have to marry him. I *loooove* big guns."

I laughed again, that odd, unfamiliar sensation and emotion.

Jolene said, "According to Gomez's scanners, our attackers have indeed repaired their tires, track systems, and engines. Them boys are powering up for an imminent attack and you need your shields. Bug shields are less likely to be seen by recon satellites than Bug weapons. I recommend you bring up shields and let the invaders expend ammunition against them for a while. That gives you time to stabilize your power levels and question the CO's prisoner. Plus, it gives the satellite time to descend below the horizon, which will allow you to use Gomez's sexy weapons systems. From the time the first satellite descends below the horizon and the time that the next one rises, you will have four minutes, forty-eight seconds to fire all weapons and go dark."

That was a tight timeline to destroy my attackers.

"Open up," Mateo said into my earbud.

I slapped the airlock open and Mateo placed a woman inside. I closed the outer airlock and opened the med-bay, scooped out the mostly-healed cats, placing the felines on Jagger's belly. Making sure the cats were out of the way, I opened the inner airlock. Dragged the woman inside. Her suit had instituted pneumatic anti-shock protocols. Mateo had not been kind to her. She stank of blood, urine, sweat, pain, and Devil Milk. I tossed the woman in the med-bay and closed the lid, setting the protocols for triage and advanced life support. I hit the office control for Level Five Decontamination. I mopped her blood from the office floor fast. She hadn't been swarmed by bicolors and bitten by a queen, so she wasn't a queen herself, like Clarisse Warhammer and me. She couldn't spread her own nanobots, but I wasn't taking chances. I'd figure out a way to use the Grabber in here as soon as I could, so I would never accidently infect another human.

"Estimated thirty-second warning until attack, Sweet Thang," Jolene said.

I threw myself back into my Com seat. "Mateo, you clear?"

"Affirmative. I am at the Grabber, tossing twenty-seven Puffers under for deactivation. With your two, that makes twenty-nine for this burst. Your cats are handy herders."

That was a lot. And . . . that meant Tuffs and the cats had understood they needed to herd the Puffers into one place. That was freaky. And kinda scary.

"Gomez, bring up shields," I said.

But before Gomez could comply, the MS Angels hit me with everything they had. The ground shook. The noise was incredible. The vibrations clattered my teeth and rattled my bones. The shields went up sparking. The noise decreased, the Bug shields absorbing and deflecting everything. Orange light filled the office.

The cats purred. Jagger snored.

The Tac Vehicles, the mini-bot, and the Mammoth moved in, toward the office. I counted the minutes and seconds for the satellite to drop below the horizon. Hoping the shields held.

The enemy bombardment continued.

I lost a lot of scrap. I lost Tesla engines, copper wiring, the newly purchased AGR Tesla, and even a stack of old cast-iron bathtubs. The barrage cost me a lot of money. But the shields held. And Mateo's suit sensors read stable. Wherever he was hiding it was in a safe location.

Over the noise, Jolene said, "Satellite declining below horizon. It will be safe to fire the B/B array in three, two, one."

"Drop shields. Gomez. Target invaders and fire B/B array."

"Roger that. Firing."

The weapons fired. A dozen blasts of dark matter particle beams swept the vehicles out front and held there, that peculiar orange glow brightening the entire junkyard. The attackers' weapons stopped. The engines stopped running. Everything stopped.

The temperature in the office went up twenty degrees in four seconds and the warning monitors began to blare. Cold night air blew in from outside through the retrofitted vents, hard blasts, the fan engines whining.

The cats went silent, all eyes on Tuffs and me.

The B/B array used dark energy—physics and tech no earth scientist understood yet, mostly because they didn't have a functional array to work with and no Bug would tell them. The only thing anyone on Earth or in the solar system knew about the particles was that they sounded like "BeeBee" in Buglish. I, however, had a Bug ship, a small one that had downed the *SunStar*. Access to the Bug ship gave me knowledge about how to operate the array, if not how it actually worked. It also made the perfect office and safe house, as long as I could keep its presence here a secret. Snug as a bug in a rug. Something Pops used to say to me when he tucked me in at night, before the war.

It took a good five minutes to fry the people in the vehicles. I had less than that between satellites. I watched as someone jumped from the Mammoth and died, his body leaping and bouncing as he boiled. It was kinda gross.

Tuffs jumped into my lap. She put her nose to mine and stared.

"I don't know how it works," I told her. "But it makes things hot, especially organic things."

It boiled them in their own juices. It didn't do much to Hemp-plaz. It didn't do much to metal except make it hot, though not hot enough to melt it, damage the temper, or warp it, or not in the short term. Just hot enough to boil and sear flesh. It was a bio-specific weapon. It damaged nothing except living creatures.

"Stay away from it until I tell you it's cooled."

Tuffs showed me images of bodies. Dead *humans*. I got the concept of *Good protein*.

"You can have the bodies once Mateo pulls them out of sight."

Tuffs made a gruff sound of pleasure and leaped to the floor to stare around at the members of her pride.

Time passed. Jagger snored. I got up from my chair and stood over him. He was huge, big enough to fit perfectly in the space I had originally called the Bug bed, though I'd no idea what the Bugs used the space for; I had dragged in an old RV bed and set it up for sleeping and under-bed storage. Every few months, I placed the quilts, pillows, sheets, and all my stinky clothes under the AG Grabber and then took them into town to a laundry while I shopped for supplies. I'd probably be charged for the cat-hair cleaning now.

It was past time for cleaning. But maybe I'd take a few nights to sleep in the bed and smell Jagger on my pillow before I took the laundry load to town. Just a few nights where I could feel less alone. I put a hand on Jagger's. His was calloused and rough and so hot it almost hurt. A cat butted my hand away and hunched her shoulders at me as if in warning. I stepped back.

Jolene said, "Next satellite will rise above the horizon in ten seconds. Nine. Eight . . ."

I retook my command seat and placed my hand over the control that worked as an off button for the shield.

". . . Three. Two. One."

I slammed my hand down. The B/B shut off.

Instantly, half-cooked people raced from the Mammoth. Mateo targeted them and took them down. It took maybe thirty seconds. Everything went silent.

Mateo spoke through my earbud.

"Initiating silent tracking in case someone got away. I'll keep watch on the wreckage. It'll take hours before the vehicles are cool enough to inspect, even by me. It'll be dawn by then and I'll drag them to the back of the property, under some ghillie-tech cloth and out of sight."

He fired another shot at something I didn't see.

"Roger that," I said. "Don't forget to eat something."

"Yes, Mom," he said, making fun of little ol' me trying to take care of warbot him.

I ended comms and spun in my seat. The cats

were all looking at me.

"Okay, that's unnerving."

Tuffs lifted her tail and walked to the storage compartment where the preserved goat milk was stored. Pointedly, she looked back over her shoulder.

"Ah," I said. "I guess you do all deserve something special. Stay away from the vehicles out front and stay off the office roof where the B/B array is. Both are probably hot."

I opened both airlocks to retrieve the cat bowls. Cats came running from everywhere. I used all the remaining goat milk, added some powdered milk and water to it, poured the last of the fish stew into a tiny bowl for Tuffs and Notch, and poured a lot of crunchy krill-based kibble—placing the extra-special treats outside, near the body of Rikerd Cotter, which was beginning to smell.

I didn't need to look at his face. Or the faces of the ones out front. I killed them on purpose because they were trying to kill me and mine. And they were all just protein now.

Tuffs made a demanding chuff, looking at the kibble and the lack of two sets of cat bowls. She sniffed in disdain.

"I'll add serving dishes and sardines to the grocery list. I haven't forgotten our deal."

I peeled the purple malleable explosive material off the door seal and rolled it all into a ball. Mateo might be able to use it someday. Back inside, I sniffed. My office smelled of cat and feverish man. Jagger was still deeply asleep, his fingers and feet twitching, his face twisted in pain.

At the med-bay, I released the hatch. I removed my protective armor sleeve and placed my bare palm on the face of the damaged female. I let my bio-nanos go to work.

After five minutes I said, "Wake up."

She didn't. So I put my other hand on her, holding her face between my palms. I could practically feel my nanos entering her pores and her bloodstream. After another five minutes I repeated, "Wake up."

This time, she did. I smiled. She smiled back.

"I'm Shining. What's your name?"

"I'm Cupcake. I'm Red's Old Lady."

"Tell me about Clarisse Warhammer. And the location of Evelyn Raymond. And the plans of the Angels. Tell me everything."

She smiled happily. She started talking.

Seventy hours and some minutes later, the entrance and the road out front were clear of scrap and bodies and anything else that might have made an uncomfortable new memory for Jagger.

Waggling his thumb and little finger at me in a gesture that was more Hawaii surfer than mainland biker, he took off on his One Rider, dust flying into the morning air. The OMW national enforcer had what he'd come for—the sensor from my kutte. He had a plausible story of what happened while he was here, believing that he had been followed by some MS Angels and that he had saved the girl—Heather—who worked in the front office from attack. The story would hold because he was mine. He'd come back when I called him, and when he did, there would be four fresh graves and parts of a tactical vehicle as evidence to support his implanted memories. The story in his mind would hold.

Well, probably. I clutched the pulse weapon he'd left with me, hoping I'd never have to use it, but grateful to have the totally illegal military weapon. A girl can never have too many weapons out here in the middle of nowhere.

His One Rider approached the road out front. He

turned and looked back.

I frowned at him. Outlaws didn't look back.

Before Jagger woke up, Mateo and Jolene had spent an entire day scanning and testing parts of the bike with special emphasis on the AntiGrav and the miniaturized Massive Particle Propulsion engine. The CO, his southern belle AI, and Gomez were happy as any tech-savvy sentient and probably-becoming-sentient beings could be.

Jagger turned to the front and pulled onto the road. As the familiar, muttered, soft snore putter of the One Rider engine faded into the distance, the cats lined up around me, sitting, watching where I watched. They looked abnormally well fed and would for quite a while. At Jolene's suggestion, Mateo had carried the cooked bodies into the deep freezer in the *SunStar*. We'd thaw a body every month or so and toss it to the cats. Sadly, Clarisse Warhammer and One-Eyed Jack had never reappeared. I was fairly sure the queen and her main mate had survived and gotten away.

She now knew I had Bug weapons.

I knew this much about Warhammer. She would never share what she knew about me or the junkyard with anyone else because she would want my stuff for herself.

She'd be back. With reinforcements. Eventually. Depending on how long it took her to convert new people and grow a new nest. How long it took to obtain equipment. And generate a plan to take me. I knew what she was. She didn't know what I was. All she knew was that I had something she wanted, something that would give her power, something that, in the wrong hands—her hands—would upset the balance of power and maybe restart a full-blown World War III, instead of the skirmishes and tech attacks and bot assaults currently taking place.

I wasn't giving up the junkyard. No way, no how.

The airlock opened, and my thrall stepped out into the sun, one hand over her eyes, searching for me.

"Go back inside," I waved at her. "I'll be back in a minute."

Cupcake, who refused to be called by her real name, waved back and followed orders. I didn't know what I was going to do with her. Outright murder wasn't something I could or wanted to do. Keeping her around was going to be difficult unless I started raiding the *SunStar*'s stores regularly. There wasn't money, water, or food otherwise and the loss of Harlan and the Tesla-23B engine had delivered a beating to my income.

I had worked to implant in Jagger's memories a desire to take Harlan's place as my boss's agent between the OMW and the local black market. Jagger had agreed, which was why Mateo had allowed him to live and leave. But I didn't know how long Jagger's compulsion would last.

I looked back at the office, focusing instead on my current short-term worry. Clarisse's nanos and my nanos in Cupcake's body might recognize each other and go to war, taking her out of the picture entirely. Not that I was hoping for that. Except for talking incessantly, Cupcake was good company.

As soon as Jagger's dust settled, the cats wandered off, except for Notch and Tuffs and the newly-named Spy—who wasn't sick with Clarisse's nanobots either. So far, so good. The cats stuck around, watching as Mateo spider-crawled to where we stood and sat, his long legs bending his main carapace to the ground so he could see me almost face-to-face from inside his meter-wide faceplate. He detached his damaged leg and placed it under the Grabber, watching me. Waiting for the conversation we clearly had needed to have for a while.

I engaged the AntiGravity Grabber. The mechanical leg lifted off the ground and hung there. Inside, the attacking nanobots fried and died. We'd done the same to each piece of his suit, one at a time, over the last three days, a method suggested by Jolene, which would minimize the time Mateo had to spend out of his suit. This was the last piece except for the torso. Next I'd need to unhook him, peel him out of the suit, and carry him into the med-bay while the whole suit got a thorough blasting, just in case the piecemeal method had left some nanos alive. I resettled my 2-Gen glasses over my not-quite-human eyes and studied Mateo.

"So. You're a spaceship captain. Commanding Officer of the *SunStar*."

"Was."

"And Evelyn Raymond? Who is probably part of Clarisse's nest and no longer has full self-will?"

"My second in command. Someone I owe." He tilted his deformed head inside his bot body, thinking. "I have self-will, and I'm part of *your* nest. She had the same training I did, so who's to say she hasn't retained some form of independence? And if she hasn't"—he heaved a sigh and shrugged, his bot-arms lifting slightly, which was weird-looking—"she'll need to be eliminated."

"Okay. I get that. So. When are we going after her?"

"Not sure yet. According to our prisoner, Raymond is hell and gone from here and we don't have much intel on the location or specs of Clarisse's nest. We're just two. You have thoughts about rescue plans?"

"Not yet, but Jolene and Gomez have become really chummy. Gomez might be Bug AI but he's a lonely Bug AI. I think they're falling for each other. And Gomez has scanners we know zilch about. He might have access to weapons or locations or . . . most anything." I grinned. "Between the AIs and you and me, I think we could take on a team of MS Angels and rescue Evelyn."

Tuffs made an outraged hiss.

"And the cats," I said. "Begging your pardon, Tuffs." She flipped her tail at me, mollified.

"And Jagger?"

"I did what you suggested and put him to work. If he follows my implanted compulsion, he'll become my new Harlan."

Even though I had planted all that in Jagger's brain, the person he would remember for the conversation was my fake boss, a burly macho man. I'd even given Jagger all of Harlan's contacts, and told him that there was a traitor to the OMW in the list somewhere, and that person also likely had access to whoever was working in the Gov. and making alliances with the Angels. Jagger had told me it was probably a cell of people, not just one. He would be breaking bones and busting teeth, to find the traitors. That was an enforcer's job and he was looking forward to it.

"And the traitors in the Gov.?" Mateo asked.

"I'll have to go after them eventually, as soon as I get intel from Jagger on the traitor cell. They made an alliance with the bloody bedamned MS Angels. There are some things an OMW would never permit to happen. Not without a fight."

"And you're OMW?" Mateo asked, a wicked grin pulling on his disfigured face.

"To the core," I said. "To the core."

About the Author

Faith Hunter is a New York Times and USA Today best-selling author. She writes dark urban fantasy, paranormal urban thrillers, paranormal police procedurals, and science fiction.

Her long-running, bestselling, Skinwalker series features Jane Yellowrock, a hunter of rogue-vampires. The Soulwood series features Nell Nicholson Ingram in paranormal crime solving novels. Her Rogue Mage novels, a dark, post-apocalyptic fantasy series, features Thorn St. Croix, a stone mage in an alternate reality. She also writes a Scifi novella series: Junkyard Cats.

Under the pen name Gwen Hunter, she has written action adventure, mysteries, thrillers, women's fiction, a medical thriller series, and even historical religious fiction. As Gwen, she was part of the WH Smith Literary Award for Fresh Talent in the UK, and won a Romantic Times Reviewers Choice Award in 2008. Under all her pen names, she has over 40 books in print in 30 countries. Faith has won numerous awards and *Curse on the Land* won an Audie Award for 2017.

In real life, Faith once broke a stove by refusing to turn it on for so long that its parts froze and the unused stove had to be replaced. She collects orchids and animal skulls, rocks and fossils, loves to sit on the screened back porch in lightning storms, and is a workaholic with a passion for whitewater kayaking and RV travel. She prefers Class III whitewater rivers with no gorge to climb out of, and drinks a lot of tea.

Some days she's a lady. Some days she ain't.

www.faithhunter.net   www.gwenhunter.com
www.facebook.com/official.faith.hunter